the Vampire Diaries

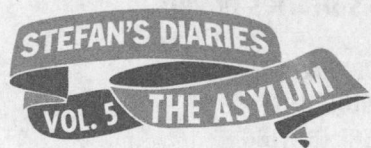

STEFAN'S DIARIES

VOL. 5 — THE ASYLUM

The Vampire Diaries novels

VOL. I: THE AWAKENING
VOL. II: THE STRUGGLE
VOL. III: THE FURY
VOL. IV: DARK REUNION
THE RETURN VOL. 1: NIGHTFALL
THE RETURN VOL. 2: SHADOW SOULS
THE RETURN VOL. 3: MIDNIGHT
THE HUNTERS VOL. 1: PHANTOM

Stefan's Diaries novels

VOL. I: ORIGINS
VOL. 2: BLOODLUST
VOL. 3: THE CRAVING
VOL. 4: THE RIPPER
VOL. 5: THE ASYLUM

The Secret Circle novels

THE INITIATION AND THE CAPTIVE PART I
THE CAPTIVE PART II AND THE POWER

the Vampire Diaries

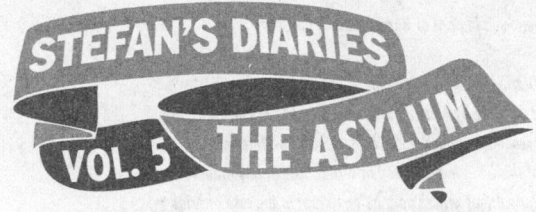

STEFAN'S DIARIES

VOL. 5 THE ASYLUM

Based on the novels by
L. J. SMITH

and the TV series developed by
KEVIN WILLIAMSON
& JULIE PLEC

HARPER TEEN
An Imprint of HarperCollinsPublishers

HarperTeen is an imprint of HarperCollins Publishers.

alloy**entertainment**
Produced by Alloy Entertainment
151 West 26th Street, New York, NY 10001
www.alloyentertainment.com

Library of Congress Cataloging-in-Publication Data is available.
ISBN 978-0-06-211395-5

Typography by Liz Dresner
11   12   13   14   15   CG/BV   10   9   8   7   6   5   4   3   2   1
❖
First Edition

the Vampire Diaries

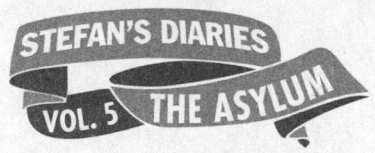

STEFAN'S DIARIES

VOL. 5 THE ASYLUM

Before someone dies, their blood races, pounding through their veins, filled with everything that makes them human—adrenaline, fear, the desire to live. It's a sound like no other, a sound I used to listen for eagerly, in anticipation of the kill. But the pounding that echoed in my ears now wasn't caused by a human heart. It lacked that frantic sensation that made blood so irresistible. It was mine . . . and my brother's.

We had both been at the very edge of death, again, and were now fleeing back to London.

The London I'd seen was a city of deceit and destruction, where innocent lives were lost, and blood ran through the streets like water. And now,

Damon and I were headed there to stop it. I only hoped the price wouldn't be too high.

Mere hours earlier, I had been attacked and left for dead by Samuel, a truly cunning and vindictive vampire. Damon had saved me. It had seemed like a miracle when my brother burst into the cottage and dragged me to safety just before the entire structure burst into flames.

But I stopped believing in miracles a long time ago. What it had been was luck. And now I needed luck on my side more than ever. Relying on instinct wasn't enough. My instincts had failed me countless times, always leading to someone's death. And if they failed me again, I knew that the ensuing death would be my own. All I could do was throw myself into the battle against evil and hope that my luck hadn't run out.

he train whistle pierced the silence of the carriage, startling me out of my reverie. I sat up, suddenly alert. We were in a first-class cabin, surrounded by every comfort imaginable. A plate of untouched sandwiches sat on the table between two plush red velvet benches, and a pile of newspapers was stacked beside them. Outside the window, the scenery rolled by, lush and full of life, the fields occasionally dotted with herds of cattle. It was hard to reconcile the calm and beauty of my surroundings with the horror and confusion in my mind.

Cora sat across from me, a small, leather-bound Bible lying open in her lap. She stared out the window, unblinking, as if the world outside could offer her the answers I couldn't. Cora, an innocent human girl wrapped up in the vampire world through no fault of her own, had just witnessed her sister turn into one of the bloodthirsty demons she feared.

Just one week ago, my life was as pleasant—I would hesitate to say as *good*—as I could have hoped. After all, being at the mercy of my cravings tempered simple pleasures like golden-hued sunsets and Sunday night dinners. But my life was peaceful. And, after years of running from my enemies and my own guilt, peace was perfection.

A week ago, I'd been employed at Abbott Manor where, as the groundskeeper, my biggest concern was whether the pasture fence needed repairing.

A week ago, I'd been sitting in a comfortable red-velvet chair in the Abbotts' sitting room, a glass of brandy on the table next to me and a book of Shakespeare in my lap. Even though I'd have to feed on the blood of a squirrel or sparrow to be satiated, I was enjoying the scent of a roast being prepared by the family's housekeeper, Mrs. Duckworth.

A week ago, I'd watched as Oliver Abbott ran indoors, trailed by his older brother, Luke. They were both filthy from playing in the forest. But instead of scolding them, their mother, Gertrude, had leaned down and picked up one of the orange maple leaves they'd traipsed in with them.

"Beautiful! Isn't fall enchanting?" Gertrude had exclaimed in delight, examining the leaf as if it were a precious jewel.

My heart twisted. Now, because of Samuel, Oliver's little body was buried under the leaves, drained of blood. Gertrude and the rest of the Abbott family—their father, George, Luke, and the youngest, Emma—had been spared, but I could only imagine the terror in which they now lived. Samuel had compelled them to believe I had been the one to kidnap and kill Oliver. It was his attempt to even a score I wasn't aware existed—I still wasn't sure how it came to be.

I squeezed my eyes shut. Damon had just left the carriage, most likely feeding on a fellow passenger. Ordinarily, I didn't like my brother's insistence on feeding on humans. But now, I was thankful for the quiet. We'd fled the farm several hours before and I was only just beginning to relax. My shoulders dropped and my heart had stopped hammering against my rib cage. For now, we were safe. But I knew London would be a different story.

I glanced at the Bible, still open on Cora's lap. It had been well read by someone; the cover was frayed and the pages were dotted with smudges. But there was nothing in the Bible that could help her—or any of us in this car of the damned.

In the distance, I heard footsteps coming down the aisle. My heart quickened. I sat up, ready to defend myself against whoever came around the corner: Samuel, Henry, some other vampire minion I had yet to encounter. I could feel Cora tense beside me, her eyes growing wide with fear. A hand reached around to pull the curtain of the carriage open. I recognized the ornate lapis lazuli ring that matched my own, and breathed a sigh of relief. It was Damon returning, his eyes wild and bloodshot.

"Look at this!" he sputtered, waving a newspaper in front of my face.

I took the paper from his hand and read the headline: JACK THE RIPPER IDENTIFIED BY EYEWITNESS. Below the block letters was an illustration of Damon. I quickly scanned the first few lines: *Society man discovered to be unholy killer. Man about town Damon DeSangue has been positively identified in relation to the Miller's Court murder last week.*

The train lurched toward London, the city that would now believe Damon was Jack the Ripper. We were like mice on our way into a snake pit.

"May I see?" Cora asked, holding out her hand expectantly.

Damon ignored her. "They could have run a better picture of me, at the very least. That illustration doesn't do me justice at all," he said sulkily as he settled onto the bench next to me and crumpled the paper into a ball. But I could see his hands shaking—the faintest of tremors, so subtle, they would be invisible to the human eye. This wasn't the confident Damon I knew.

Cora rifled through the papers lying next to our untouched breakfast trays.

"We're only a few miles outside London," I said, looking at Damon. "What will we do when we get there?" For all we knew, we'd be apprehended as soon as the train arrived at Paddington Station.

"Well," Damon said, throwing the wadded-up newspaper to the ground and stomping on it for good measure. "I've heard the British Museum is exquisite. I haven't had a chance to see it yet."

"This is serious, Damon. They're looking for you. And once they find you . . . " I shuddered, thinking of what would happen if the Metropolitan Police found Damon.

"I know it's serious. But what am I supposed to do? Hide for eternity because I'm being framed for a crime I didn't commit? Samuel needs to pay. Besides, I'm not afraid of the police. I may have a few tricks up my sleeve."

"You're in this one, too," Cora said quietly, holding up the front page of the *London Gazette.* This article had no illustration, only a headline: JACK THE RIPPER DISCOVERED, STILL ON THE LOOSE.

Damon grabbed the paper and quickly scanned it. He turned to me. "The press has labeled me a nobleman. I look like a pauper now, so I doubt anyone will recognize me," he said as if to convince himself. Lacing his fingers together, he smoothed back his hair, then rested his head in his palms as if he was a sunbather at the beach.

It was true: He didn't look at all like a member of London's elite. His shirt was torn and dirty. His eyes were tired and bloodshot, and he had the shadow of a beard covering his chin. But he still looked like Damon. His hair was dark and thick, falling in a wavy line over his strong eyebrows, and his mouth was set in his usual half-sneer.

Catching me looking at him, Damon arched an eyebrow. "I know you're thinking something. Why don't you just say it?" he asked.

"We shouldn't be going to London," I said flatly. After all, Damon was a wanted man in the city—a weak, friendless wanted man at that. We had no idea how many other vampires were allied with Samuel. His brother, Henry, was one for certain, but we could only guess how far Samuel's reach extended. He certainly must have had friends in high places to frame Damon in the media.

"Not go to London?" Damon spat. "And do what? Live in the forest and wait until we're found? No. I need revenge. Aren't you concerned about your little friend, Violet?" he added, knowing that was exactly why I was after Samuel in the first place.

I looked at Cora, desperately rummaging through the papers as though one of them contained a map to safety.

Her blue eyes were wide with fright, and I was struck by how well she'd held herself together after last night's events. She'd been brave in the hours before sunrise, when we'd been hiding in the woods and waiting for the search party to pass, despite the fact that her sister had just been turned into a demon. Now, I could only imagine the thoughts swimming in her head.

"I want to rescue Violet. I do," I said, hoping that Cora could sense my sincerity. "But we need a sound plan. We don't know what we're up against."

Even as I said it, I knew Damon would never agree. When he wanted something—romance, Champagne, blood—he wanted it now. And the same applied to revenge.

Out of the corner of my eye, I saw Cora set her jaw. "We have to go to London. I wouldn't be able to live with myself if I didn't try to save my sister," Cora said, her voice rising on the word *save*. She folded the paper with a crisp smack and pointed to another illustration. I flinched, expecting to see Damon. But instead, it was a drawing of Samuel, his chin held high and his hand raised in a poised, political wave.

"Let me see that," Damon said, snatching the paper from Cora's grasp.

"'Samuel Mortimer, the hopeful London councilor, vows to keep the city streets safe. "I'll kill the Ripper with my bare hands if I have to," Mortimer promises, to cheers of approval,'" Damon read from the text. "I'd like to see him try."

I winced. Samuel *Mortimer*, derived from the French word for dead. Of course. And neither I nor Damon had realized it, even though Damon was so proud of calling himself Count DeSangue. Count of Blood. It had probably been Samuel's first clue to Damon's true nature.

I shook my head. What other hints had we missed? Hadn't I fallen into Samuel's trap, too? I'd believed Damon was the Ripper.

"Promise you won't do anything until Violet's safe," Cora said. "And then, yes, kill him. Just don't let Violet be a pawn."

I didn't want to make Cora a promise I couldn't keep. I wasn't even confident that Damon and I could defeat Samuel, but I knew Damon wouldn't pass up any opportunity to try. I wanted to tell her to run away from all of this, as far as she could. Go to Paris, change her name, and try to forget the past. But she wouldn't. Violet was her sister. Cora was bound to her, just as I was bound to my brother.

I gave Cora a slight nod, and for her, it seemed to be enough. I rubbed my eyes, trying to wake myself up. I felt as though I was drunk, or trapped in a dream. Everything that had happened in the past twenty-four hours had taken on a hazy quality, as though I had dreamt the events, not lived them. But this was real.

The fields outside were becoming fewer and farther between, and the air had taken on a grayish, murky quality. Whether I liked it or not, we were nearing the city. In the distance, a flock of swallows flew in the opposite direction of the train, toward the open country and the sea beyond it.

"Don't worry. We'll find Violet," I said hollowly. I hoped I could teach Violet the ways of drinking animal blood, of quenching cravings, of living with a constant hunger, the way Lexi had taught me. I hoped it wouldn't be too late.

A grandfatherly conductor with wiry gray hair pulled back the curtain and walked into the cabin. He tipped his hat and smiled kindly at Cora. I wondered what we looked like to him: three siblings on an outing? Two young lovers and a chaperone? I took comfort in knowing that in his wildest dreams, he'd have no way of guessing our true natures.

"London, next stop!" he announced, his look growing suspicious as he noticed Damon's bloodstained shirt. This wasn't the conductor we had compelled to obtain our first-class carriage car, and I could tell from the way he pursed his lips that he was seconds away from asking to see our tickets.

Damon turned toward him and arched an eyebrow.

"Thank you," he said in a low voice. A small smile appeared on his face as his mind melded with the conductor's. In seconds, the conductor was completely under Damon's spell.

I watched, impressed by how easily Damon could compel, even when he was wounded and half starved. When I compelled, I was often left with a headache and a sour taste in my mouth. Damon seemed to suffer no such side effects.

"You'll leave us alone from now on. We've shown you our tickets. You never saw us," Damon said, his words smooth and even.

Cora watched Damon, clearly curious as to why the conductor was hanging on his every word. She opened her mouth and I started to shake my head, worried she'd break the compulsion. But she only whispered to Damon: "Have him give you his hat."

Damon glanced at her, bemused. "And I need your hat," Damon said in the same smooth tone he'd been using the whole time.

"Of course, sir," the conductor said, handing it over.

"And the jacket," Cora urged, raising an eyebrow.

"The jacket, too," Damon said. I watched, impressed. It was as if Cora were compelling Damon.

"Very well," the conductor said, shrugging off his dusty gray uniform coat and neatly placing it on the seat next to

Damon. He shuffled out of the coach in his shirtsleeves, the curtain falling closed behind him.

"That was good thinking," I said. I hadn't met a human so comfortable with vampires since . . . well, since Callie. I shook my head, trying to dispel the image of the girl I'd once loved. Callie was the past, and the only thing I could do now was focus on the present.

"It was necessary. His face is plastered all over the paper. At least we didn't have to ask for worse." Cora shuddered, and I knew she was thinking back to her own compulsion, when Samuel had forced her into becoming his blood slave. "Damon, as soon as you get off the train, put those on. No one will look at you twice if they think you're a railroad man. It's not foolproof, but it'll have to do," Cora said, nodding to herself.

"Thanks," Damon said begrudgingly as he tried on the hat. Far too big and sliding over his eyes, it was the ideal way to hide his features. "Ladies always do such a good job of finding the most appropriate outfit for the occasion."

Cora's mouth twisted as though she was resisting the urge to smile. She had already spent quite a bit of time with Damon, back when she was being compelled by Samuel. I imagined she'd gotten used to his dark, occasionally sarcastic humor.

"I know where we can go," Cora said. "At least for a bit."

"Do you? We'd be most obliged if you shared that

information with us," Damon said in an exaggerated show of politeness.

Cora leaned toward us, resting her elbows on her knees. Her arms were spattered with blood from tending to my wounds.

"Once we get off the train, just follow me," Cora instructed, keeping her voice low and glancing at the cabin door. "I can't tell you where. I don't want anyone to hear. We can't be too careful. Isn't that right?" Cora asked, her tone challenging Damon to disagree.

"Well said," Damon muttered acquiescently. I was pleased by Cora's foresight and her ability to manage my brother. She may have seemed innocent and naïve, but she had a backbone of steel.

Cora nodded tightly and went back to looking out the window. I studied her. In addition to the crusted blood on her arms, she also had red splotches on her blue cotton dress. From a distance, it looked the fabric was patterned with roses.

The train whistle blew three short blasts. We were minutes from the station.

"Grab your coat," Cora reminded Damon, as though she were a mother speaking to her child on a snowy day.

Damon shrugged his shoulders into the oversize gray jacket, which looked almost like the Confederate uniform he'd worn more than two decades ago.

"Good," Cora said. "Now, Stefan, take up the rear and make sure no one notices or follows us."

"Of course," I said abashedly. I'd thought we'd have to protect Cora, but it seemed Cora was protecting us. Did this dependence on a human to lead us to safety mean we were worse off than we thought? Or was Cora the good luck charm I'd asked for? Either way, I trusted her.

2

oon enough, the train chugged into Paddington Station, trailing a cloud of black smoke.

The three of us moved swiftly and stealthily off the train and through the bustle of the platform. As we headed toward the exit, my eye landed on three policemen huddled in the center of the station. One turned toward me, his gaze resting on my face for a moment before moving on to scan the rest of the crowd. My shoulders relaxed. No one was suspicious of us.

The area surrounding the station was a world away from the ornate buildings Damon preferred, all gilt and gleaming marble. These buildings were crowded together and boarded up, and no one seemed to be around. The air felt heavy, as if it held all the city's dirt suspended around us.

Dark clouds were gathering overhead. "Looks like it's going to rain," I said. I shook my head as soon as I said it, disgusted with my attempt at small talk. I sounded like a farmer talking to my neighbor.

Simple Stefan, I imagined a smooth, dulcet voice teasing. I shook away the thought of Katherine.

"I suppose so," Damon said in his maddening noncommittal drawl, as though he was still in Virginia and had all the time in the world.

"Are you boys just going to stand there, or are you ready to follow me?" Cora asked, putting her tiny hands on her hips.

Damon and I glanced at each other and nodded. "We're ready if you are," Damon said.

Cora quickly got her bearings, then took off through the winding, sprawling streets of West London toward the sludgy, slow-moving River Thames. I used to think the Thames was majestic, flowing into the Atlantic Ocean and connecting London to the world. Now, it looked murky and malevolent. I followed a few steps behind Cora, alert to any signs of Samuel, outraged citizens, or the Metropolitan Police. Every so often, I'd see a tumble of chestnut-brown curls cascading down a slim back and would glance quickly away. Even now, when I had so much on my mind, Katherine haunted me.

As we continued to walk along the river toward the

pedestrian bridge across the Thames, familiar sights of London loomed before us. I could see the domed chapel of St. Paul's Cathedral, and farther down, Big Ben. Beyond that were warehouses that abutted the river. The warehouses where Samuel had held Cora under compulsion and where Violet had been turned into a vampire. London was a study in contrasts, with the church spires that reached toward the heavens masking the hellish underbelly that we were steeped in.

Soon, we found ourselves on the Strand, the street closest to the Thames and one of the city's commercial epicenters. I caught a few people staring at us suspiciously. I wasn't surprised. In our bloodstained, dirt-caked clothes, we looked worse than the beggars who often hung about the city squares.

"We're almost there," Cora said, also sensing the sideways glances of passersby. She smoothed her dress, put back her shoulders, and marched across the bridge without a backward glance.

"She's a good one to have around," Damon observed as he fell into step beside me.

"She is," I agreed. For once, my brother and I were on the same page.

On the opposite bank, Cora neatly turned down a set of winding stone steps leading to the edge of the river. The area under the bridge housed nothing apart from a giant hole in the ground, covered over with wooden planks and iron beams. This must have been a construction site for an Underground station. I remembered George Abbott telling me about these trains. The plan was to connect all of London via a web of underground train tunnels. The city's goal was to have a functional line by the turn of the century. But judging by the state of the hole, the crew wasn't in any hurry. The area looked abandoned.

I trailed behind Cora like an obedient puppy as she picked her way through the site. A KEEP OUT sign was tacked on a nearby post and a low post and wire fence surrounded the hole. Some worker had made a halfhearted attempt to cover the opening with a sheet of canvas, but I could see the top of a thin wooden ladder poking out. Cora stopped nearby.

"It's not exactly the Cumberland Hotel, is it, brother?" Damon asked wryly.

She ignored Damon's quip, focused on the task at hand. "We can get down this way," she said, climbing over the makeshift fence.

"But is it safe?" I asked skeptically. How did Cora know how to sneak into the Underground?

"Of course. Violet and I slept here once, so if it's safe enough for two women, it should be safe for any vampire," Cora said. Her voice had a teasing edge to it.

"You slept down here by yourselves?"

Cora shrugged. "We didn't have any money. We promised to pay the boardinghouse as soon as we had jobs, but they kicked us out. I knew we shouldn't sleep on the streets, so we used to walk all night. We'd start by the Ten Bells and then make our way over to here. We'd follow the river and tell each other stories to pass the time. We'd let ourselves rest as soon as it got to be light. But then one night, Violet was near delusional with exhaustion, and we found this," she explained, gesturing to the tunnel. "It's shelter, and when you're friendless and surrounded by enemies, there's no place better," she said, arching an eyebrow at Damon as she yanked the canvas back and swung one leg, then the other, onto the ladder. She clambered down into the darkness, quickly trailed by Damon.

"Wait!" I called, but there was no answer. Just as I stepped onto the first shaky rung of the ladder, I heard a sickening thud from below.

"Cora?" I called out desperately as I quickly climbed deeper into the pit. "Damon?"

"Here!" Cora said. "I'm all right. Just mind—"

I took a step, expecting to feel a rung below my feet. Instead, my foot fell through air, and I landed with a thud on my back.

"—the drop." Cora's voice cut through the darkness.

"I'm fine!" I said, quickly standing and brushing myself off. I let my eyes adjust to the light. We were in a cavernous tunnel that sprawled out in all directions. I could hear water dripping from an unseen source. I could also hear the faint sound of breathing, far off in the distance, although I couldn't be sure it wasn't merely my overactive, paranoid imagination.

Damon's eyes glittered in the darkness. "Well, you've told me often to go to hell. I believe we've arrived, haven't we, brother?"

"I think this is the ideal place to hide. But if you don't like it, you can leave. I can find my sister by myself. I'm used to doing things on my own," Cora said stonily.

"You don't have to," I said. I wasn't going to abandon Cora. I owed it to her to keep her safe. I may have failed her sister, but I wouldn't fail her.

"Stefan's thrilled to help you," Damon said sarcastically. "Now, I'm going to excuse myself. It's been a terribly exciting day, and I must rest," he said as he sauntered deeper into the tunnel.

"Don't you want to go, too? I'm fine by myself," Cora said, stepping toward me.

"No, I'm staying with you," I said firmly.

"Well, then, fair warning, I'm not the best company right now." She walked a few paces away, where a man-made ledge was carved into the dirt wall. She climbed up and swung her legs back and forth. She looked more like a girl sitting on a porch swing at a summer barbecue than a woman surrounded by vampires, hiding out fifteen feet below sea level.

"Cora . . . " I began. I wanted to let her know how much her sister had meant to me. "Even though I only knew her for a few days, I thought of Violet as a sister and . . . "

Cora sighed. "I'm tired, and I'm sure you are, too. Please, can we just not talk?"

"Of course," I said quickly. I settled on the hard dirt floor. Not talking was probably for the best. Whenever I got too close to humans, something terrible happened. It had happened with Callie. It had happened with Violet. It had even happened with little Oliver. And I couldn't let it happen anymore. And yet, I couldn't help but want to comfort Cora in any way possible. After all, she must be terrified. If she kept all her emotions locked inside, they'd end up overwhelming her. I knew that all too well.

I squeezed my eyes shut so tightly I could see stars on the insides of my eyelids. If Lexi were here, she'd have suggested a cup of goat's blood tea to feel better. If Lexi were here, I probably wouldn't have gotten into this situation in the first place.

Stop it, I said to myself. Feeling sorry for myself wouldn't help matters. I needed to sleep. But lately, every time my eyes closed, my mind drifted to the root of my problems. How I'd become who I was now. I'd close my eyes, eager to untangle a complicated web of thoughts and emotions, only to be interrupted by the image of her porcelain face. *Katherine.* Her large, doelike eyes. Her lips, parting, ready to . . .

Sc-ratch, sc-ratch. My eyes shot open. A rat was burrowing next to me, its beady eyes practically glowing in the darkness. Instinctively, I reached out, snapped its neck, and drank its blood in large, quick gulps.

It was as foul as a pool of standing water, but it was something. Blood of any kind still had an intoxicating effect on me, tapping into a primal part of my being that I'd tried to suppress.

It was only once the blood was rushing down my throat that I became aware of my surroundings again, and remembered Cora was only a few feet away. Pulling the dead animal from my lips, I leaned closer to her. Her breathing was as steady as ever. She must be asleep. Relieved she hadn't witnessed my true nature, I laid back down, trying to find a comfortable position on the ground.

And then a voice cut through the darkness like the light from a candle.

"I hope you enjoyed your dinner." Cora. But she didn't sound frightened. Instead, she was equal parts curious and concerned.

I felt shame rising like bile in the back of my throat, mingling with the acrid taste of blood from the rat. I wanted to tell her I was sorry, that I hadn't meant for her to see that. "Good night," Cora said, as if my midnight snack had been nothing but a glass of warm milk.

I listened to the echo of her voice in the empty tunnel. "Good night," I finally whispered back.

But she didn't answer.

3

hroughout the night, I could hear the clawing of rodents and the endless dripping of water. London seemed miles away, when, in reality, it was only a hundred or so feet above me. But despite the distractions, I somehow fell into a deep, dark sleep.

... Until I felt that familiar paranoid tenseness—someone was watching me. I opened one eye, then another. A pale blue eye looked back. Scrambling backward and instantly fully awake, I realized I was mere inches from Cora.

"What are you doing?" I asked roughly, running my tongue over my teeth, relieved to find that they were short and straight. As I stood, I heard the sickening crack of my joints. I may not have aged in two decades, but a year of living on the Abbott farm had softened me; I was no longer used to sleeping on the hard ground.

Cora's face fell. "I'm sorry," she said, sitting up and pulling her knees to her chest. She smoothed the fabric of her skirts down over her legs. "I got frightened." Her red hair was matted on one side of her head, and there were dark circles under her eyes. Her skin was sallow, and her lips were cracked. It was odd to see her so vulnerable, after she'd been so strong the previous night. It was evident that she needed a friend. And truthfully, so did I.

"It's all right," I said, softening my voice. "Sometimes I just don't trust myself."

"Well, if you can't trust yourself, then who could trust you?" Cora asked, her piercing gaze boring into me. "Besides, I don't think I'll ever be safe," she said ruefully.

An uncomfortable silence fell between us. Beyond the sounds of dripping water and scrambling rodents, I could hear a symphony of human sounds from far off in the tunnel: coughing, limbs creaking, a steady thrum of hearts pumping blood through bodies. Our immediate vicinity was deserted, and I knew Cora couldn't hear our neighbors like I could. But we weren't the only inhabitants of the Underground. I wondered if that was why Damon had been in such a hurry to leave us.

"He's feeding, isn't he?" Cora asked, reading my mind.

"Most likely," I said. I sat back on the ground, the dust settling around me. In the darkness of the tunnel, it was impossible to tell whether it was night or day. Not like it mattered much. Without a plan, we were in limbo.

"You saw me feed last night." It was not a question.

Cora nodded. "I heard the snap of bones breaking, so I looked over. It wasn't terrible. Not so different than watching some of the men at the Tavern slurp soup. You don't frighten me, Stefan," she said, as though it were a challenge.

"Does Damon?"

Cora shook her head, a faraway expression in her eyes. "No. Maybe he should. But he doesn't. If anything, Damon . . . what's the opposite of fright?" Cora asked, biting her lip.

"I suppose the opposite would be comfort," I said, mystified as to how we'd gotten into this thread of conversation.

"Comfort . . . no, not that," Cora mused. A small smile appeared on her pale face. "I think you're more comforting, even if you are very destructive to rodents. Damon keeps me . . . sharp. He makes me think. I feel like there's an edge to him, and you always have to be at the top of your game. I never would have thought of him stealing the conductor's clothes on my own. It only came to me when I was watching him."

"It was a good idea," I said, thinking it was she, not Damon, who was sharp. She'd known about this tunnel, after all.

"Well, thank you. I only hope I keep coming up with them," Cora said, smiling slightly. Then she turned away. "Do you think Violet is drinking human blood?"

"Yes." There was no reason to sugarcoat the subject. If Violet was with Samuel, she most certainly was drinking human blood. The only uncertainty was who her food supply would be—a compelled blood-slave or some poor soul soon to be considered another one of Jack the Ripper's bloody conquests.

"What's it like?" she asked, whispering even though no one else could hear us.

"It's . . . " I paused. What *was* feeding like? I'd spent decades trying to forget. But as soon as she asked, I remembered the warm, rich taste of human blood. Of course, I wanted to say that it was terrible, that Violet wasn't enjoying it, and that she'd stop as soon as we were able to find her and pull her out of Samuel's clutches. But that wouldn't be true.

"It's like nothing anyone could imagine unless they've tried it. I suppose it's like coming into a firelit room after spending a night sleeping in the rain." I had no idea where the comparison came from, but it was remarkably apt. Human blood made me feel whole, warm, alive in a way that animal blood didn't.

"So . . . why would anyone stop?" Cora asked.

I shrugged. "A lot don't. But there are benefits to

abstaining from human blood. I can still feel things, feel emotions like I could when I was human. The need for blood, the thirst, can become so overpowering that you have to shut them off when you're feeding so you don't think of the consequences. But without it, I don't have to feel like a monster, or get lost in the darkness. When I see Violet, I'll explain it to her. But for now, take comfort in the fact that she's nourished, and she's not in pain."

Cora shook her head in disbelief. "I can't imagine her ever hurting a living thing," she said quietly. "There was once a field mouse that had gotten into the house, and my mum was all set to kill it. Violet was about eight at the time, and she cried and cried until my mum set it loose. Vi even used to put out food for it, just in case it came back and was hungry." Cora's voice broke and she covered her face with her hands. "I just want to find her!" she yelled, the sound muffled by her fingers.

"She's not here, that's for certain." Damon strode out of the darkness, wiping his mouth. He was still wearing his blood-spattered clothes from the night before, but there were no longer dark circles under his eyes. Under the circumstances, he looked incredibly handsome. Cora dropped her hands to her lap and stared at him.

"Did you find your breakfast?" Cora asked tersely, her hand unconsciously brushing against her neck. An image flashed in my mind: Samuel, hunched down, fangs bared over Cora's smooth skin. I wondered how often he had fed on her. And it might have been my imagination, but I thought I saw two tiny scars, small and round as pinheads and waxy pink in color, midway between her shoulder and her ear. I shuddered.

An inscrutable expression crossed Damon's face. "Yes, I did," he said simply. "At first, I was simply making sure the tunnel was safe. And it is safe for us. There are a few souls down here, although none that will bother us. Everyone here is pretty bad off. It was rather easy to feed."

"So that's what you did all night? And here I thought you might be coming up with a grand plan. Meanwhile, you were gorging yourself," Cora said sternly. "I hope you catch a disease from one of these tunnel dwellers. It would serve you right."

"I won't, Miss Cora," Damon said, shifting from one foot to the other. "But I wouldn't be surprised if Stefan here made himself sick. I'm sure he's told you all about subsisting on bunnies from the forest, but look where he landed: the same place as me, stuck underground, the target of a vampire who needs to be cut down to size. There are ways to feed on humans and still care about them," Damon said pointedly.

I clenched my jaw and locked eyes with Cora. I wanted her to stand up for my beliefs and choices. I wanted her to remind Damon that not long ago, she'd been the one providing a blood supply to vampires. But instead, she merely looked disappointed.

I paced away from Damon, knowing the worst thing I could do was jump into a fight. The peace we'd brokered after he'd saved my life yesterday was fragile at best, and I knew from experience how one simple word said in anger could turn us back into enemies. And we already had one enemy to contend with.

I massaged my temples. The fetid, cloying dampness of the tunnel felt far too much like being entombed. "I think I need some fresh air. Cora?" I asked, offering my arm, knowing full well Damon couldn't come with us when his face was in every major London newspaper.

"Enjoy yourselves. I think I'll just continue to drink in the life down here," Damon said, flashing me a crooked smile. He knew I was excluding him.

Cora glanced between us before moving to join me. Once we reached the ladder, I steadied her foot on my palm to boost her up. I followed behind, politely averting my eyes to avoid looking up her skirts. In the daylight, the ladder was much less intimidating than it had seemed the night before.

We emerged into the still-deserted construction site. I pulled my pocket watch from my trousers. A dent near the crown flashed me back to the moment when Samuel had shoved me against the wall of my cottage. Still, the watch ticked steadily. Unlike its original owner, Mr. Sutherland, it seemed to be indestructible.

Half past nine. Around us, the city was noisy and bustling. As we walked up the winding steps from the embankment, I noticed men in waistcoats hurrying in and out of the formidable stone buildings rising up on either side of us. The cobblestone streets were clogged with pedestrian traffic, and a man carrying a newspaper bumped into my shoulder but continued to walk without turning. No one paid any attention to Cora and me, and I was glad of that.

My shoulders sagged, and I realized the enormity of my relief. It was as if the tunnel had exacerbated all my nightmares and made me assume destruction was imminent. Yes, my brother and I were in grave danger, but London was the same as I remembered. Carriages rattled over cobblestone streets, peddlers were hawking flowers or nuts or newspapers, and men offered their arms to ladies. Nothing was different and yet . . .

"*Read all about the latest murder!*"

I whirled around. On the corner, a skinny boy was crowing the day's shocking headlines, convincing the passersby of their need for a newspaper. His voice cracked with excitement every time he yelled the word *murder*.

My stomach tightened. Cora and I glanced at each other. "I should buy one," I said, rummaging through my threadbare pocket for change. Finally, I found two pennies caught in folds of the fabric. I hadn't thought of money as we were fleeing. Now, it was just another advantage Samuel had over us. He had access to riches that allowed him to effortlessly grease the wheels of the machines that ran London. Meanwhile, we would have to lie, compel, or sneak our way around the city.

I paid the newsboy and shoved the folded paper under my arm. I didn't want to read it yet. I wanted to get away from the crowds, away from the tunnel.

Together, Cora and I drifted to the shady side of the street.

"Do you have a destination in mind?" Cora asked, pulling me out of my thoughts.

"I thought we'd go to the park. It's a good place to . . . talk," I said, my eyes darting suspiciously from left to right as if to see if anyone was following. No one seemed to be watching us.

"Good idea," Cora said. "But first, I need breakfast. Shall we try that place?" She gestured toward a red awning of a bakery at the end of the block.

"Of course," I said, shielding my eyes against the sun. We'd reached a calmer, more residential area of London. Townhouses lined the winding streets, and elm trees shaded the cobblestones. Far off in the distance, I could make out one of the lush green hills of Regent's Park.

I opened the door of the bakery and was immediately overwhelmed by the yeasty smell of baking bread. My stomach turned. When I was hungry for blood, the scent of human food always made me feel slightly queasy.

"What can I do for you, dears?" A short, squat woman leaned over the counter and smiled welcomingly at us. Her arms were as large as Christmas hams, and for one second I imagined her warm, sweet blood on my tongue. My stomach growled as I locked eyes with her, concentrating on her dark pupils.

"We'd like you to give us a bag of buns. And a loaf of bread. Actually, two loaves," I said. The less compelling I had to do, the better. If she could provide enough food to last Cora a few days, that would be ideal.

The woman nodded slightly as I felt my request seep into her mind, felt her will begin to bend to my suggestions.

"And a strawberry tart," Cora piped up.

I repeated Cora's request to the baker. She bustled around behind the counter, finally handing me a large paper sack, steam still rising from the loaf on top.

"Thank you," I said, and we left the bakery before she could second-guess the strange transaction she'd just made.

The closer we got to the park, the more the scene reminded me of the Impressionist paintings that were so popular in Paris. From a distance, the trees looked lush and green, but up close I saw orange and brown leaves about to fall to the ground and muddy patches of heavily trodden grass.

"Would you like a roll or your strawberry tart for breakfast?" I asked.

"I'll have a roll. The tart's for later," Cora said as we walked through two imposing marble pillars marking the entrance to the park.

"Here," I said, placing one of the still-warm rolls in Cora's outstretched hand. "I apologize for the lack of jam."

"I don't mind," she said easily, picking apart her roll. A tiny shower of crumbs fell to the ground. Instantly, five sparrows converged on the spot, pecking furiously.

As we moved deeper into the park, there were fewer pedestrians and nannies out with their charges than there had been at the entrance. Sun dappled the white gravel path beneath our feet, and every few steps an errant leaf from the oak trees above us wafted to the ground. I wasn't sure what had brought me here. This was the last place Violet would be; she couldn't be outside in the daylight, not without a lapis lazuli ring like the ones Damon and I had. I wished that, somehow, I could just *know* where Violet was, the same way I used to be able to sense where Damon was on the Veritas estate where we'd grown up. But Damon was of my blood, a bond I would never have with anyone else in my eternal life. It was the same type of bond that kept Cora in the company of vampires, a desperate attempt to get her sister back in any way possible.

Suddenly, Cora perked up and whirled around. "Look!" she called, pointing past me.

I squared my shoulders and followed her gaze, ready to see a police officer here to take us away, or worse, Samuel. But what Cora had seen, just a few yards away behind a metal fence, was a giraffe gracefully stalking around a pen.

Cora clapped her hands in delight. "Violet and I always walked this way on our day off. We called it the cheap zoo tour. The admission counter is on the other side, but why would you pay admission if you can just watch from here?" Cora stood on her tiptoes and shielded her eyes. I followed her lead and spotted two camels feeding at a trough. I took a step closer to Cora, drawn by her innocent curiosity.

"Which is your favorite?" I asked. For the moment, it was nice to be in the sunlight, having a normal conversation.

Cora stepped closer and leaned lightly on the iron fence. "I like the zebras, but Violet always liked the peacocks. She was drawn to their dramatic flair . . . " Cora trailed off wistfully. "Sometimes you can see them. But not today," she said, disappointed. She turned toward me and took another bite of her roll.

I remembered how pleased Violet had been when she picked out a gorgeous emerald-green dress from Harrods, and how she seemed to sparkle with infectious enthusiasm at the few parties I'd attended with her.

"Violet always wanted to be an actress. We both did," Cora said, turning away from the zoo. Her gaze was focused on her feet, clad in filthy white shoes. "But I think Violet could have made it. I wanted to meet exciting people and have a few years of adventure, but I didn't necessarily want to be on display. Violet wanted people to notice her. She wanted to be special."

"She was special," I said after a moment.

"I guess now she's special in a different way," Cora said sadly.

"I did everything I could to protect her . . ." I said.

"I know," Cora said, reaching up to touch the vervain necklace still clasped around her throat. "You gave her this."

"Yes, and it—"

"Protects me against vampires," Cora finished. "Damon told me. I just wish . . . " She trailed off and reached into the bread bag to take another roll. It was evident that there were certain things Cora kept to herself, a wall around her thoughts. I knew the feeling. Sometimes the privacy of my own mind was the only thing that kept me sane.

"We'll find her. I'll make sure of that," I said finally, knowing as soon as I heard the words that it somehow wasn't enough.

"Will we?" Cora asked, turning her gaze on me. "You keep saying that, and I know you mean well, but it seems you and your brother are rather occupied, what with trying to one-up each other." She tossed the remaining crumbs from the roll toward a lone pigeon hopping down the path. It startled, then began to feast, pleased at this meal from the heavens. "I'll save her by myself if I have to. After all, she was trying to save me. It's what sisters do," she said in a vulnerable voice at odds with her jutted chin and proud expression.

"I know," I said. "But you won't have to do it alone. I'm here to help."

Cora took a deep breath and looked into my eyes. "I know. And I trust you. I trust Damon, even. But when you're both together . . . " She trailed off and shook her head.

"My brother and I have a . . . complicated relationship. As you've seen. But we're on the same side. We're not fighting each other anymore."

A brief smile crossed Cora's lips. "Good," she said. We'd walked the length of the zoo and were entering a rougher section of the park. Litter was strewn across the grass, the paths were cracked, and fewer well-dressed couples wandered by. We passed a group of children, but instead of playing with expensive wooden toys, they were improvising war games with sticks.

I watched as two boys, probably only five or six, tussled violently. Both had bloody scratches and I couldn't help but wonder whether that was how Damon and I seemed to Cora: brothers so desperate to fight, they didn't care how childish, counterproductive, or useless it was.

Just then, I heard a commotion behind us. A dark-haired figure ran by us at a speed no human could possibly match. Five officers followed, not caring about the people they knocked down.

I grabbed Cora's hand. She was looking at me in fear, knowing just as well as I did what this chase meant.

Damon was in the park.

"Danger!"

"Killer!"

"Stop him!"

Almost unbidden, a word bubbled to my lips as I watched Damon flash across the landscape: *Run!*

4

he Ripper!" boomed one officer as he rushed by in panic.

"The Ripper?" A crowd had gathered and I heard someone take up the officer's cry. Another followed suit, and soon the park was full of voices raised in a cacophony of fear. People were running this way and that, as though they were a flock of sheep who'd discovered a wolf in their midst.

"I see him!" another officer yelled, swinging a club in the air and taking off toward a grove of trees. I watched in horror. Damon was fast, but this was broad daylight. It would only take one person in his path to slow him down long enough to be caught.

To ensure Damon had enough time to escape, I knew I needed to create a distraction. "Help! Police! Help!"

I shouted, an idea forming in my mind. I grabbed Cora's waist and pulled her close to me.

"Pretend you've fainted," I whispered under my breath. "Help!" I called louder.

An officer running by slowed and turned toward us, his eyes flickering with suspicion.

"My sister fainted!" I called, allowing my voice to break a bit for dramatic effect. Playing along, Cora had gone heavy and limp in my arms.

Two more officers halted, and I breathed a sigh of relief. Seconds were paramount, and I was hoping this pause would give Damon time enough to escape. *Why* had he left the tunnel? He knew he was on the front page of the paper. He knew Jack the Ripper was the name on everyone's lips. Why was he always tempting fate?

"Boys, keep going. I'll tend to this," the first officer ordered, charging at me. The other policemen took off in Damon's direction, but the ruse should have gained him thirty seconds on them. Time enough to put significant distance between himself and his pursuers.

"Please, come quickly!" I continued, my voice ragged as the officer puffed up the hill toward us. I felt Cora's sides involuntarily contract and knew she was laughing at my admittedly terribly overacted performance. "Please help!"

The officer leaned over to inspect Cora, and she stilled.

"Probably just fright," he said, prying her eyelids apart with his pudgy fingers. At that moment, Cora righted herself unsteadily.

"What's happening?" Cora asked, fanning her face with her hand. "I heard the Ripper was here, and I just . . . why, fear must have overtaken me." Cora blinked her large eyes up at the officer.

"Yes, ma'am, you fainted," the officer said sternly as he fished a handkerchief out of his pocket and rubbed it over his sweaty, moon-shaped face. He was in his late forties and looked like he'd rather be chasing the Ripper than dealing with a hysterical young woman. "You shouldn't be out here, even with your brother. A murderer is on the loose!"

"Oh, thank you for protecting us," Cora said. "I don't know how to repay you, except to pray that you catch the Ripper soon, Officer . . . "

"Officer Evans," he said gruffly, tipping his black hat at her. "And I don't want to be rescuing you again!" he called over his shoulder as he jogged down the hill. The rest of the police had disappeared into a patch of trees, and I only hoped Damon had outrun them all.

Cora turned toward me, her blue eyes wide, the flirtatious expression she'd given the officer wiped from her face. She looked deadly serious. "We need to go back to the tunnel and find that idiot brother of yours."

I nodded, pressing my lips together. If Damon knew what was good for him, that's where he would hide out until this all blew over.

I grabbed Cora's hand, acting as if we were just out for a stroll. Cora squeezed it, and together, we made our agonizingly slow way through London's winding alleys. The streets smelled like sewage and rotting vegetables, and the cobblestones were covered in a thin layer of water. I tuned into my vampire senses, picking up the *whoosh* of blood coursing through millions of bodies. But nowhere did I hear Damon.

Instead, what I heard was fear. I couldn't help catching strains of conversations between passersby.

"Said he fled London, but what good does that do? Still means the Ripper's terrorizing our country."

"And for the killer to be that well-off? Shows money doesn't buy common moral decency."

"My bet is he's back on the town and will be terrorizing again tonight."

"I'm telling you, any man who allows his wife out of his house after dark is asking for trouble."

"What are you doing?" Cora asked curiously.

"Sorry." I straightened up and shook my head abashedly. Concentrating on the conversations wafting past us had pushed me into full-on hunt mode. My head was cocked, my jaw set, and my eyes were flicking back and forth across the crowd. "People are talking about the Ripper."

"Of course they are." Cora set her mouth in a firm line. "All of London wants him dead. I know Damon thinks he can outwit everyone, but he cut it really close. Let's just hope he learned his lesson today."

"He hasn't learned it in twenty years," I mumbled under my breath.

Cora whirled around sharply, and I knew she'd heard me. "Stefan Salvatore, I bet there're some lessons you still need to learn, too."

I nodded. "That's true," I said quietly. I liked Cora's spirit.

When we got to the tunnel, I took the lead in climbing down. Even from the fifth rung, I could hear the scurrying of the rats, as familiar a background noise to the tunnel as cicadas had been on June days back in Virginia. But underneath that I heard an angry sigh that I'd recognize anywhere.

"He's here," I said in relief, taking off into the dank tunnel.

Finally, after a few twists and turns, I found Damon, sitting in a dark corner, illuminated by the glow of a makeshift fire. His hair flopped over his forehead, his dark eyes were bloodshot, and he was reading a well-worn paper. Stubble covered his face, and he looked every inch the outlaw he now was.

"Samuel's killing me," Damon said, looking up from the fire. "He has single-handedly made sure that I cannot go anywhere in London. I even wore the disguise. *That* worked well," Damon said in disgust, throwing the gray conductor's hat on the fire. A plume of smoke rose up.

"Why did you go out at all?" I exploded. "You know you're being watched. You're the biggest news story in the country!"

Damon shrugged. "You don't get anywhere without a little risk. People barely looked at me when I was wearing the conductor uniform. And it wasn't as if I was sightseeing. I was trying to find Samuel, do the dirty work so you wouldn't have to. Instead, I got chased down like a common criminal." Damon shook his head in disbelief. "Of course, those police officers had nothing on me. I felt sorry for them, huffing and puffing like that."

"They almost caught you. You're welcome, by the way," I said angrily. If we hadn't distracted the officers and given Damon the space he needed to dash into the woods, who knew where he'd be by now?

"That was *you*? *'My sister fainted!'*" he lisped, mocking me. "Well, that was highly unnecessary. I was fine."

"You could have gotten yourself killed," Cora said sternly.

"It's either kill or be killed in my world," Damon replied tersely. "And I intend to kill Samuel for this. After all, he's the one who concocted this Jack the Ripper nonsense. And then to attach my name to it! As if I'd ever be so sloppy." Damon fumed. "He can't face me himself, so he sends humans to do his bidding. And if that isn't enough, I read this little item in the paper. The fool's having a party tomorrow night to announce his political aspirations. Let's consider this our invitation. His party will be his funeral," Damon said ominously. The hair on the back of my neck bristled. If there was one thing I knew about Damon, it was that he always followed through on his convictions.

"Do you think he's compelling the police?" I asked. "Or do you think they recognized you from the paper?"

"How would I know?" Damon asked, throwing his hands up in disgust. "It's not like I'm privy to his master plan. I thought he was just another London aristocrat, someone I could use to introduce me to the right people. I never imagined he was a vampire with rage issues. If anything, he should have been thrilled to have found another one of his kind. But now, he's running me out of my city, and I won't have it."

"What about Henry?" I asked. "What do you think his motive is?"

"Whatever Samuel says," Damon spat. "Henry's a useless sap who follows Samuel around like a farm dog. Not unlike another brother I know."

But before I could come up with an insult of my own, Cora piped in.

"So who is Samuel, really? Is he that important?" she asked.

"Samuel's running for London councilor. I was helping him plan his campaign," Damon said, a twisted grin forming on his face.

"Well, then we need to come up with a plan to stop him. We've already wasted a day." The one thing I'd learned in my two decades as a vampire was that inaction always seemed to backfire. Biding my time and waiting for the perfect moment to strike had never worked. I'd always been late by a minute, an hour, a lifetime. But no more.

Damon smirked. "Stefan saves the day. What a brilliant idea. 'We need to find him.' Well, that's what I was trying to do."

"You can't just run around London hoping you'll run into him!" I fumed. That was Damon's problem: He acted on impulse, rarely considering consequences. It was a trait that worked when besting humans. But Samuel was a vampire and stronger than both of us combined. Our only hope was to outwit him. "We have to be strategic. Maybe it's good he's in the spotlight," I said, thinking out loud. "It means he has to work that much harder to hide certain things."

"He's good at hiding things," Cora said softly, fingering the vervain charm around her neck.

"Do you remember anything else about Samuel?" I asked urgently.

"Think I didn't already ask her that, brother?" Damon interjected. "She doesn't remember anything. She only recalls the warehouse parties. I was the one in his inner circle."

"I can speak for myself, thank you!" Cora interjected. But when she didn't continue, it was clear she didn't have any further information on our enemy.

Damon's lip curled as he pivoted toward me. I could see sparks from the fire reflected in his pupils. "Let's pay him a visit," Damon said.

"Pay him a visit," I repeated flatly. "Just show up on his front steps? When you're a wanted criminal? Have you forgotten that we have to be invited into a home by its owner? I doubt Samuel will extend the courtesy." It was one of the many things that differentiated us from mortals: In order to enter a residence, a vampire had to be asked to cross the threshold. It was a small restriction, but one that meant some places were still safe from monsters like us.

"Thank you for the etiquette lesson, brother. But I don't need to go inside. All I need is to speak with Samuel, man to man. Or, should I say, vampire to vampire," Damon explained. "I'm done playing cat and mouse. And I'm not going to leave London without a fight," Damon said, clenching and unclenching his fists.

"A fight to the death?" I asked pointedly. In New Orleans, when Damon and I had been forced to battle each other underneath a circus tent, our fight had been billed as such. We'd only been saved when Callie started a fire that brought the tent down. Did Damon truly have such a short memory?

"Yes, a fight to the death," Damon repeated, seemingly oblivious to my allusion. "But a proper one. No surprises, no using humans, no games. Just the two of us against each other. I'm going to go to his door and get the answers. And then, I'm going to destroy him."

"Let me get this straight. You're going to head to his house and *invite* him to fight? He didn't exactly offer the same courtesy when he tried to kill me," I said incredulously. It was dramatic and over the top and so *Damon*. But while a duel was romantic, he didn't have a chance of winning. Not in his state. I tried to imagine the way Damon's plan would play out. Samuel may not anticipate us ringing his doorbell as though we were guests. He could be caught unawares, in front of people who didn't know his secret, and he'd be forced to keep his cover. After all, I doubted he'd stake us in a roomful of London's political elite, nor could he compel them all simultaneously. Still, the plan was rife with problems. I knew I couldn't talk Damon out of it, so the best I could do was be there when it fell apart.

"Yes, let's go. But answers first, duel later," I said wryly. I wasn't surprised he'd gotten on Samuel's bad side. The question wasn't what he had done, it was what he'd done *this time.*

"You gentlemen have fun on your fact-finding mission," Cora said. "I'll head to the Ten Bells. With Samuel occupied, it'll be the safest time to ask if any of the girls have seen Violet."

I didn't like the idea of Cora going off on her own, unprotected. But she was right; it was safer for her to be in Whitechapel than to come with us to confront Samuel. The look of determination on her face warned me not to argue.

"Fine," I said after a moment. "I'll go out for supplies. I'll be back soon." I walked down the tunnel without a backward glance, my footsteps echoing against the packed dirt. Every move I made caused a wave of scurrying rats, and I wondered if they knew how futile their frantic search for safety was. Were they oblivious to the fact that if someone really wanted to, they could be killed in an instant? Or, in their tiny minds, did they think of themselves the way I was beginning to think of myself—as a walking target, simply awaiting the moment of my doom?

* * *

A few hours later, I arrived back at the tunnel, my arms laden down with two suits, several shirts, a pink silk dress, and a lavish petticoat. I'd returned to Harrods, where Violet and I had shopped to replace our torn and dirty clothes so we could blend in as best as we could. As soon as I'd entered the store, several salesmen had gathered around me eagerly, like vultures feeding on a carcass. By the time I had finished shopping, I was so drained from compelling the crowd of salespeople that I hardly even knew what I was carrying.

As soon as I had my goods, I'd made a hasty exit, intent on feeding. Eventually I'd found a malnourished pigeon on a deserted street, but was still famished after draining its blood.

The sound of laughter echoed in the tunnel.

"Hello?" I called curiously.

A response ricocheted back to me. "Back so soon, brother?"

I turned the corner and saw Damon and Cora, sitting opposite the fire from each other. Cora had an animated expression on her face, and her eyes were gleaming.

"I brought clothes for you," I said, placing the clothing—hundreds of pounds' worth of finery, which I'd gotten for free—in piles on the dusty ground.

"Thanks," Damon said. He leaned over and began

picking through the piles, finally pulling out a black wool cloak. I'd thought it might help him to blend into the night. He straightened up and tossed the rich fabric around his shoulders. "You outdid yourself. This cloak makes me look like one of Gallagher's finest magicians. Don't you agree?"

I smiled tightly. It was an apt description of the outfit. Gallagher's was the terrible circus where, as vampires, Damon and I had been held captive and forced to fight each other. We were the only authentic acts. Everything else, from the tattooed woman to the conjoined twins, had been the result of two-bit trickery.

"You don't look bad, brother," I said.

"No, he doesn't." Cora smiled appreciatively. "Well, I'm off to the Ten Bells, before either of you can stop me. I'll have you know that I don't need a man *or* a vampire to protect me," Cora said, standing up and flouncing down the tunnel into the darkness.

"Now, there's a girl you wouldn't have met in Mystic Falls," Damon murmured, clearly impressed by her independence.

"Probably because no girls like that would have wanted to meet you. They'd have had the good sense to stay away," I shot back, even as I wondered what Damon meant. Was Cora becoming a romantic interest for Damon? There was no way that could end well.

"Their loss," Damon said easily. He threw the hood of the cloak over his head, concealing his face. "Anyway, brother, let's focus on the task at hand. It's a lovely day for a family hunt, wouldn't you say?"

5

'd gotten used to my life stretching in front of me, as vast as an endless ocean. But in the past two weeks, my worldview had constricted. Now, working our way through the alleyways and darkened streets of London, all that mattered were the next few minutes and hours. Would we kill Samuel? Would Samuel kill us? How would he react to discovering I wasn't a pile of ashes back at Abbott Manor? And were we about to enter into a death match with the undead?

Damon seemed to hope so. In fact, he was treating the entire ordeal as if we were soldiers going into battle, and it was his duty to muster the troops. The only time his mood seemed to lift was when he described the ways he wanted to destroy Samuel.

Eventually, I tuned him out, allowing him to continue

his monologue about whether he'd stake or burn Samuel, or both.

Damon and I hurried along empty streets toward Samuel's Montague Street home, darting this way and that to avoid any suspicious glances. Not like there were many. In our new outfits, with the bloodstains finally washed off our skin, we looked like two wealthy young men enjoying everything London had to offer. We certainly didn't look like hungry creatures of the night, about to do business with the devil.

We turned onto Montague in silence, walking under the hazy gaslights dotting the street. Down the block, carriages were rolling up to a large, well-kept house blocked from the view of pedestrians by an ivy-covered fence.

I turned to Damon, but he was distracted, leering at a stylish woman leaning tipsily on the arm of her companion. She was wearing a blue dress that left her lily-white neck exposed and vulnerable.

Damon arched a dark eyebrow. "Lady Ainsley," he explained as he watched her carry on with a man who was clearly not the Lord Ainsley I had met. "Not as faithful to her husband as he'd hope."

I turned to Damon in the darkness, a revelation forming in my mind. "Do you think that's why Samuel's angry? Jealousy?"

"Did I take one of his women, you mean?" Damon

asked. "I didn't take anyone. They were all more than happy to go with me."

Lady Ainsley and her escort turned and walked up the gaslit path toward the house.

"Well? Let's go," I said, gesturing at their retreating backs.

"Yes," Damon agreed, but he seemed lost in thought. I wondered how many of the women at the party he'd known, how many business deals he had struck with their husbands. Samuel could be holding a grudge for dozens of reasons. Damon always went after what he wanted, not caring who was in his way. Fallout was inevitable when it came to Damon's conquests, and unfortunately I wasn't stranger to getting wrapped up in it.

"Penny for your thoughts, brother?" Damon asked, easily catching up to me.

"You don't have any money," I joked. "All you have is the cloak on your back, and I was the one who stole that for you."

"True. But I have other ways of making you talk."

"I was thinking that you make enemies more easily than friends," I said as we made our way toward Samuel's home.

I surveyed the expansive grounds. From the street, it looked more like a park than a private home. The four-story Georgian mansion dwarfed the redbrick houses on either side. A main path, lit up by candles, led to the front door. Several smaller dirt paths wound around the house and through groves of maple and elm trees. I shook my head in disbelief. How was it that Samuel could be a vampire, could kill at will, and still live here, with the respect and admiration of humans? Meanwhile, I'd spent the past two decades trying to do the right thing, surviving on whatever scraps I could find, always afraid to get too close or ask for too much.

My mind drifted to our estate back in Virginia. It had been called *Veritas*, Latin for "truth." My father had named it, adamant that a man's primary purpose in life was to search for truth and fight deception. Maybe it was a path that worked for humans. But for a vampire, seeking the truth often meant unwittingly causing death. If I'd left the Jack the Ripper murders alone, Oliver would be alive. Violet would be human. But Cora would still be enslaved by Samuel, and countless more girls might have died. Damon would have been framed by Samuel and might have been hung by the police. No matter what path we'd taken, people would have perished. It was just a question of who.

I sneaked a glance at Damon. He, too, was staring up at the house, his jaw tight.

"Well, this is it," Damon said, walking closer to the iron gates. "Moment of truth. You can either be a coward and run back to your little human girlfriend, or you can follow me. It's your choice."

"I'm not your enemy, Damon," I said. "Samuel is. Remember that."

Silently, we followed an elderly couple up the winding path to the large oak doors of the Mortimer mansion. The woman in front of us was clad in a glittering red dress, while her husband was wearing a tuxedo. It was impossible to tell whether they were royalty or vampires, and I realized that, if we were let in, the entire evening would play out like a macabre costume party, with none of us knowing the demons from the humans.

The door was opened by a well-dressed butler just as the elderly couple reached the entrance. "Lord and Lady Broad," the man said, inclining his head slightly. The butler ushered them in. I craned my neck, trying to get a glimpse inside the lavish marble foyer.

And then I spotted Violet. She looked nothing like the half-dead girl I'd last seen in Ivinghoe. She was wearing a green velvet dress, and her hair was pinned in an elaborate mass of curls. Her lips were bright red, and her eyes seemed wider than ever. She was beautiful—but I'd already known that. What startled me was the way she carried herself, shoulders thrown back, chin lifted. Gone was the aura of a fragile fawn in a forest. Now, she seemed like a lioness— beautiful, graceful, and wholly confident in her Power.

Even as she sipped champagne and smiled politely at her conversation partner, her eyes were scanning the crowd. I wondered who—or what—she was looking for.

Damon stepped into the triangle of light from the open door, pulling at his collar to reveal his face. His jaw was set, determined, and his eyes were lit with passionate rage.

"I'm Damon Salvatore," he announced himself, dropping his sobriquet. "And I need to speak to Samuel. Alone."

"I'm afraid you can't come in," the butler said firmly. His steady voice and unflickering eyes made it clear that he'd been compelled by Samuel.

"We're business acquaintances of Mr. Mortimer's," I lied. I thought of Violet, crouched over Oliver's body, being forced to feed after resisting for so long. I thought of Samuel, smiling down at me as he staked my stomach. I thought of all the destruction he'd wrought on London, of the smell of blood on the cobblestone alleyways. I thought of it all until I felt hatred begin to burn, as real and tangible as a brand pulled from the fire. I gazed into the butler's eyes, willing my hate to be strong enough to override Samuel's compulsion.

"Let us in," I growled, and felt his resolve begin to weaken. *Good.* "Now," I emphasized, not daring to blink.

But the butler stepped back and firmly crossed his arms across his chest.

"You are not to come in," he said resolutely. "And if you continue to ask, I shall have to alert my master. Or, if you prefer, the Metropolitan Police," he said, lowering his voice until he was speaking barely above a whisper. "In fact, the commissioner is inside right now, and I'm sure he'd love to see you, *Count DeSangue*."

I flinched at the way the butler dropped Damon's alias. Damon's expression remained impassive. "If Samuel's not willing to let me in, then tell him to come out. And as for the police commissioner, by all means, send him my way. Although blood on sandstone might be tricky to clean," he said ominously, raising an eyebrow.

Murmurs rustled behind us, and I realized a crowd of guests had built up as we stood blocking the door. The butler cleared his throat and smiled tightly, as if to reassure the other guests that nothing was amiss.

"I'm afraid seeing Master Mortimer is impossible," the butler said quietly, his voice tight behind his smile. "This is a private party, and you must get off the property immediately."

"Samuel always invites too many people," one of the guests complained, honking his bulbous red nose into a monogrammed blue handkerchief.

"You know you have a future councilor when commoners start crashing the party," came another voice behind me. Laughter rippled through the crowd, and my spine stiffened. I knew we had to turn around, but I wasn't ready to admit defeat. Not when Violet was so close.

"Beckford, is there a problem?" Suddenly, a presence loomed behind the butler. It was Samuel, dressed in a perfectly tailored black tuxedo. His blond hair glowed in the light shed by the lanterns surrounding the door. Hatred boiled in my veins at the sight of him. It was all I could do not to tackle him to the ground and hold him down so Damon could stake him.

His thin lips curled into a sneer at the sight of Damon and me.

"Well, well, well . . . not a pair of guests I expected to see. Beckford, I'll deal with the riffraff. How will anyone trust me as the councilor of the city if I can't handle the trouble on my own doorstep? Consider this a campaign demonstration!" He smiled widely at the crowd. "The rest of you, please come in and enjoy!" He threw his arms out in a gesture of welcome as guests squeezed past us and into the expansive mansion.

As the guests streamed in, two hulking men stepped outside, standing like bookends beside Samuel. I watched them warily. Were they vampires? Or were they human guards, unaware of their employer's true identity? One of them caught me staring and took a warning step toward me. I clenched my jaw and flexed my fingers, preparing myself for what was sure to be an impossible fight.

Once the last guest was inside, Beckford closed the door with a thud. Samuel glanced back and forth between us. I shifted from foot to foot, trying as hard as I could to seem calm. After all, I'd gotten into battles with vampires before. I'd even thrown Samuel's brother off a train. It wasn't as if he could stake us on his front doorstep. Could he?

"You two." Samuel shook his head and let out a long, low laugh. "Stefan, I would have thought you'd be in ashes by now. Or drowning in self-pity."

"If you're going to kill me, you'll have to try harder," I said, anger boiling inside me. "And I don't know what you and your brother have against us, but I want answers. We *both* do."

"Or else what?" Samuel asked calmly. "You're on my territory, so my house rules apply. And I don't appreciate trespassers, especially when I'm otherwise engaged. What did you think you would do here? Stake me? Have a bloody vampire battle while the band plays a waltz?" And that's when I saw it. Under his white dress shirt was a pendant, gleaming in the moonlight. I glanced reflexively at my own ring. It also sparkled, as if sensing its nearby match.

Samuel must have noticed my gaze because he jerked his tuxedo jacket into place and crossed his arms. But he was too late. The sparkling blue stone told me everything

I needed to know: His hatred of us had something to do with Katherine.

"Neither of you is as smart as I am," Samuel continued. "And judging from this arrogant display, neither of you has any idea who you're dealing with." Samuel glared at us as though he were a headmaster and we were his wayward pupils.

"And you're more naïve than we thought. Because this is just the beginning," Damon said in a low voice.

"Oh, I know it is," Samuel said, smiling like a cat with a mouse under its paw. "Because now I have a lovely deputy. Violet is a grand girl. Thank you for introducing us."

Out of nowhere, Damon threw a punch. It landed on the side of Samuel's nose.

Samuel blinked, but the blow had done nothing.

Samuel shrugged. "Just more fodder for the eventual flames of your undoing. As you can see, I'm unbreakable."

Damon laughed, one short bark. "You're a coward. I was coming to ask you to settle this once and for all, man to man. But you're no man," Damon spat. "Your days are numbered." With that, Damon spun around and walked away, his footsteps hard on the path.

"Remember to vote!" Samuel called at Damon's retreating back.

I had to do something. Maybe, with Damon out of earshot, it would be easier to reason with Samuel. Once I had

Violet, I doubted I could persuade Damon from acting on his revenge fantasies, but at least I'd no longer have to be part of them.

"Samuel, let Violet free. She's—" I began.

"A very hungry vampire," Samuel interrupted. "And a lovely girl to have on my arm. Now, Stefan, I'm going to let you in on a secret. I hate you. But I abhor your brother. Play nice, and I may let you off easily. A stake to the heart next time. Simple. No torture. Or maybe—" Samuel leaned toward me. The sweet scent of blood hung in the air around him; he must have fed recently. "Maybe I'd let you go completely. Just leave London. Forget about your brother. And forget about Violet. But I wouldn't count on it. After all, as I say to my constituents, I'm the type of person who gets things done." He laughed maniacally before pushing me so forcefully I tumbled down the steps and cracked my head against the path.

The door slammed shut. In the distance, I could hear another group of guests working their way toward the mansion. Had Samuel somehow used compulsion—or something else—to make sure we'd been entirely alone during the course of our conversation? And if so, what *couldn't* he do?

I stood and brushed myself off, rubbing the back of my scalp.

A short man in a top hat and tailcoat grabbed my arm.

I whirled around, fangs bared. "What?" I growled, realizing just how much Samuel got under my skin as I saw the startled expression of the stranger. I needed to stay in control.

The man shrank back. "I'm sorry. I wanted to . . . is the Mortimer house?"

I nodded, giving a slight apologetic smile.

"Thank you," the man said, fear flashing in his eyes as he rushed away.

Damon was waiting just inside the fence, pacing against the iron trellises. "I hate him. I want to pull him apart, limb from limb, in front of all his fancy guests. Just wait until they realize their precious councilor-to-be is a bloody murderer. It would serve all of them right to be killed."

"Damon, listen to me," I said urgently, leading him away from the property. "I noticed something tonight. His necklace. Did you see it?"

"No, I wasn't paying attention to his *jewelry*," Damon said as we hurried into the street. Mist swirling beneath the gaslights cast a ghostly shadow on his face. I pulled him away from the light. It wasn't safe for him to be seen.

"He had a necklace like our rings," I said pointedly. Finally, realization flickered in Damon's eyes.

"Katherine," he said finally.

The name hung between us, as palpable as the cobblestones under our feet. A shiver crept up my spine.

"He must have known her. He *must* have," I said. I twisted my ring around my finger. The inside was tarnished, and there was a slight crack in the stone from one of the many bloody battles Damon and I had fought. But it was my lifeline to normalcy—and Damon's, too. Without our rings, we would be bound to the darkness, unable to walk in the sun without bursting into flames. Damon's ring was darker and even more tarnished, the silver nearly black. But the stone was just as blue as mine. As blue as the stone in Samuel's necklace.

Damon nodded, a faraway expression on his face. I knew in his mind, he was back in the carriage house in Mystic Falls, Virginia. He was curling a lock of Katherine's hair around his finger, planting a kiss on her porcelain cheek, or arching his neck in just the right way to allow her to . . .

I stopped imagining.

"Do you think . . . did Katherine ever mention Samuel?" I asked tentatively. A coach drove by, its well-dressed passengers most likely on their way to Samuel's house.

Damon shook his head. "Katherine never mentioned any other man to me," he said sharply. The end of the sentence went unspoken: *Even you.*

"She never said anything to me, either. Have you seen a stone like that anywhere else besides on our rings or Katherine's necklace?"

"What does it matter?" Damon asked angrily, his voice piercing the night air. He threw up his hands. "All it proves is that the three of us shared the same dead vampire." He kicked at the ground, sending a shower of pebbles further into the street. He lowered his voice. "I'm more of a man and more of a beast than Samuel ever was, or ever will be. And I want him to know that." He turned on his heel and walked back toward the house.

"What are you doing?" I called.

Damon whirled around. "To hell with planning and plotting. I'm going to do exactly what I should have done in the first place. You were right, brother. Vampires can't be trusted."

"No!" I lunged at him. His expression was one I'd seen countless times. It was the same look he'd worn when he killed Callie and when he announced his intention to kill the Sutherland clan. He was out for blood, and I knew that if he attacked Samuel now, he'd be the one to end up dead.

But before either of us could make another move, we were interrupted by the crash of a door slamming shut. A girl wearing a jewel-encrusted blue dress stumbled out, blinking confusedly. I sniffed the air. I could sense her blood was wine-heavy, hear her heart beating errati-cally.

She walked unsteadily toward the line of coaches

arranged like children's models around the vicinity of the property.

Damon let out a low whistle in the darkness. I grabbed his arm and dug my fingers into his flesh. What was he doing? Now was not the time for Damon to fulfill his urges.

The girl turned around, wavering on her feet as she looked around for the source of the noise.

"Sarah!" Damon called. "Over here!"

"Do you know her?" I muttered under my breath, not sure which answer would be worse.

"Just watch," Damon whispered through gritted teeth.

The girl stumbled toward us, her hands smoothing her skirts over the curve of her hips. "Why, I'm not Sarah . . . " she said, trailing off as her gaze landed on Damon's rich clothes. "Although I could be, depending on who's asking. It's dreadfully boring in there," she pouted.

Damon bowed. As he righted himself, he swept his cloak around him with a flourish, masking his features. "Deeply sorry to misidentify you. I'm Lord Fox," he invented. "And you are?"

"Beatrice!" she hiccupped.

"Of course. Beatrice," Damon said in an exaggerated show of politeness. "You will forgive me, but in this light, you looked like Sarah de Haviland."

"The actress?" Color rose in the girl's chipmunklike cheeks. "Oh, I'm not, but she *is* inside, if you'd like me to get her. Or maybe you'd enjoy getting to know me just as well?" she asked boldly.

Damon winked, acting as if he and Beatrice were the only people in the world. I watched, transfixed. Damon had more tricks up his sleeve than simple compulsion.

"I'd love to get to know you. But first, let's play a little game. I want to play a prank on my friend Henry, who's inside right now. Will you do me a favor? Flirt with him, and get him to come outside with you? But make sure you don't mention me—I want it to be a surprise."

Beatrice smiled, revealing an unfortunate crooked incisor. "I love surprises!" she said, clapping her hands together. "I'll get him right away."

"Terrific. And once I return to the party, I'd be honored if you'd dance with me," Damon said, taking Beatrice's hand and giving it a kiss. She blushed even more deeply and quickly turned away, eager to do Damon's bidding.

"Oh, and Beatrice?" Damon called.

"Yes?" The girl whirled around.

"My favorite dance is the waltz," he said with a wink. "Remember that." Beatrice practically skipped back into the estate.

"So now what's the plan?" I asked impatiently. I'd last encountered Henry during our battle atop the train, and I had no desire ever to see him again.

"I guess you'll find out," Damon said, his fingers twitching as if he were craving a fight. I watched him nervously. Part of me wanted to tell him I wanted nothing to do with this half-baked scheme, wish him luck and then walk away. But I couldn't. At this point, there was no turning back.

Before I could second-guess my commitment to Damon, Henry and Beatrice stumbled outside. Henry was trying to pull Beatrice in for a kiss. His red hair was neatly slicked back, but his shirt was coming untucked, a sign that he'd been enjoying the party. When I'd first met him, I imagined him to be eighteen, an oversize schoolboy on the lookout for fun. Knowing his true nature made his youthful appearance all the more disconcerting.

"Come on, sweetheart, just a little taste," Henry said to Beatrice, oblivious to our presence.

Beatrice just laughed. "Sorry, my dance card for tonight is already full," she teased as she slipped back into the party, giving Damon a parting flirtatious smile.

Just then, Damon flew toward Henry at vampire speed. He grabbed Henry by his broad shoulders and shoved him against the wall of what seemed to be an abandoned stable. Henry writhed in Damon's grasp, his fangs growing and flashing in the moonlight.

"I need a stake!" Damon growled. I grabbed the first

branch I could find on the ground and cracked it over my knee. It was willow, not nearly as substantial as I'd hoped, but it would do. It would have to do.

I charged toward them, the stake in my hand. In my mind's eye, I remembered the way Henry had charged toward me during our bloody fight on board the train to Ivinghoe. I remembered the proprietary way he'd allowed his hands to roam down Violet's curves during a party at the warehouse. I remembered the way he'd eagerly clapped Damon's back at a park picnic, as though they were nothing but loyal friends. He had betrayed us.

"This ends now," I hissed, holding the stake inches from the snow-white shirt that covered Henry's chest. I imagined what the fabric would look like, pierced by the willow branch and stained with Henry's blood. I'd never really staked a vampire before. At Gallagher's circus, I'd once been forced to run a vervain-laced stick through Damon, but I'd deliberately missed his heart. This was different.

"Don't kill him yet," Damon said, wrapping his fingers around the branch. "He needs to talk first."

I held the stake out toward Damon. It may have been my battle, but it was my brother's war, and I wouldn't stand in his way.

"I don't talk to trash," Henry said petulantly. Instantly, Damon launched the branch forward and pierced Henry's throat. Blood bubbled at his throat, but the wound quickly healed when Damon removed the stick. Henry must have fed recently.

"You disgust me," Damon spat.

"Well, I can assure you the feeling's mutual," Henry gurgled, hate evident in his eyes. "And you wanted me to talk, so I'll talk. You and your brother are both stupid and impulsive, and have no idea who you're facing. Is that what you wanted to discuss?" He smiled as he pulled a handkerchief from his pocket to wipe the blood off his neck. An owl hooted in the distance. Where were Samuel's bodyguards? Could this be a trap?

As I was about to voice my fears, Henry twisted out of Damon's grasp.

"You think you can kill me? That's rich," he said as he smiled at us. "You boys will try anything, won't you? It's the American way, I suppose." He circled around us like a dog, sniffing a stranger that crossed his path. I watched every step, my entire being ready to attack, should it be necessary. "If at first you don't succeed, try, try again. Although I think, in your case, 'If at first you don't succeed, try and die again' might be a bit more accurate." Henry chuckled at his own joke.

"What does Samuel have to do with Katherine?" Damon asked, his voice low. I could see him struggling to control his temper. I wanted nothing more than to pick up where he left off and fight Henry to the death.

But Henry continued, unconcerned. "It *is* unfair to be hunted without knowing why, isn't it? After all, it's so much more enjoyable if your victims can take some time to ruminate on their choices. So, why do my brother and I hate you?" He paused and pretended to think. "Well, for one, you two are awfully pushy. In this country, we value people who respect our social rules. And that does not include elbowing one's way in with compulsion and lies. So there's that."

"What about Katherine?" I interrupted.

"Katherine," Henry said, chuckling to himself. "Well, Katherine's a category unto herself. One of a kind. The type of girl you see once and remember forever. Which is why my brother can't forgive either of you for killing her."

"I didn't . . . " Damon sputtered.

"That's not what we heard," Henry said in a low voice. "I knew the move to America wouldn't be good for Katherine. Samuel knew. But she was insistent, and when that girl got an idea . . . " He shook his head and snickered ruefully. "It was supposed to be temporary. She called it her 'Grand Tour,' a chance to see the world and live a bit before she settled down," Henry said, glancing toward the main house. "My brother was devastated when she didn't return. He loved her. And I love him, so I'm going to do whatever it takes to help him take his revenge. Is that clear?"

"She would never have returned to Samuel," Damon said, disgust evident in his voice.

"Oh, but she would have," Henry said, a sly smile on his face. Was it true? Had Katherine simply been biding her time in Virginia? Every statement Henry made brought up more questions. "She was going to make her name in America, and he was going to lay claim to London. Then, they'd combine their fortunes. But of course, they'd also have their fun. United, the two of them were unstoppable. You couldn't tie them down. They were ambitious, beautiful, and powerful." Henry sighed. "And then you ruined it."

"How about I help you both by putting you out of your misery? I'll kill Samuel, so he can join Katherine in hell," Damon growled, his eyes narrowing. They were pacing around each other as I looked on, forgotten for the moment. This truly was Gallagher's circus ring all over again: two vampires pitted against each other, and only one would survive. As much as I hated to admit it, Damon's odds didn't look good.

"Don't you want to hear more? I haven't told you how Katherine used to write letters to my brother, laughing about the two country bumpkin boys she'd met in Virginia," Henry taunted.

Damon lunged at Henry and threw him to the ground.

"Katherine loved me," he screamed into Henry's face. But Henry only chuckled. Then, with incredible force, he pushed Damon off him and against a tree. In a flash, Henry had Damon's wrists pinned to the trunk. He reared his head back and spat in Damon's face.

"Katherine would have killed you eventually, you know. That was always her plan. And now, it seems I have to finish her job."

Gathering my strength, I surged forward and pushed Henry away from Damon, intending to get him to the ground. But he was stronger than me, and shrugged out of my grasp as easily as slipping out of a cloak. The two of us stood facing each other, panting with exertion. His arm hung limp by his side, and I felt a jolt of surprised satisfaction. At least I'd managed to injure him.

"I'm not wasting my time with you right now," Henry hissed, cradling his elbow. He turned to head back into the party. "Try to have better manners next time. And that, of course, includes not staking your hosts," he called over his shoulder.

Damon stood. "Coward. Let's go, brother. I'm not going to waste my energy on that twit."

Together, we turned and walked into the darkness. Damon strode ahead, clenching and unclenching his fists. I knew he was deeply disturbed by Henry's story. He'd loved Katherine. He still did. Saying her name was the only thing that could bring a far-off expression to his eyes and stop him in the middle of a sarcastic diatribe.

"Are you all right?" I asked, putting my hand tentatively on his shoulder.

He shrugged me off. "I will be. Once Samuel's dead."

Katherine Pierce was a gruesome vampire, never hesitating to drink from a stranger—or a lover. So why could I still remember the feel of her lips against mine? And why was I suddenly obsessed with whether or not she and Samuel had been together? Katherine had such a hold on my brother and me, even with her body long since charred and buried. Which one of us would have to die for her spell to finally be broken?

Lately, I've been remembering things I thought were lost long ago. When I was fifteen or sixteen, I started dreaming of a girl. The dream always took place in a verdant field that looked like the far corner of Veritas, where the rolling green hills met *the forest. She always seemed a few paces beyond my reach, separated from me by a dark, murky cloud. The girl's face was always hazy, but I could see her straight, long, brown hair and her olive skin. Even unable to see her clearly, I knew she was beautiful.*

When I met Katherine, I thought I'd finally found her, the girl I'd been dreaming of. The one who filled me with unrelenting desire and longing. But as I slowly came to discover the monster Katherine truly was, I knew in my heart she wasn't the one.

I still held out hope. Maybe, right now, I was being tested. Maybe when I finally found her, I would be worthy of her love, that girl of my dreams.

I didn't speak to Damon during our walk back to the tunnel, and he didn't speak to me. Tension lay thick between us, and I knew we were both thinking of Katherine. There was nothing to distract us from our memories. The streets were deserted; most people were staying inside after dark, afraid of meeting the Ripper. The clock had struck midnight along our walk. I used to love this time of night. It was a time to hunt, a time to let my thoughts unpack themselves, a time to feel the world slowing down. Now, I felt like we were the ones being hunted. After all, Samuel would retaliate—it was inevitable. But when?

Finally, we reached the embankment.

"Home sweet home," Damon wisecracked as he stepped onto the ladder and began the climb down into the tunnel.

My mood turned as soon as I reached the bottom and saw firelight dancing on the opposite wall. A petticoat was strung across the tunnel, creating a makeshift wall, and a rusty, dented teakettle was balanced precariously over the fire.

"Welcome home!" Cora said, spreading her arms wide. Kohl rimmed her eyes and she'd pulled her red hair into a high bun on top of her head. She wore one of the dresses I'd brought, which made the most of her small frame.

For the first time that evening, I felt like things might actually be all right. Cora's hard work reminded me of a fairy tale my mother used to read to us, about Snow White, a beautiful princess forced into hiding amid dwarves. This version was much more sinister, but Cora played her part admirably: the kind woman trying to tame our savage tendencies.

"Did you see Violet?" Cora asked urgently. "I asked around at the Ten Bells but Alfred hadn't seen her. And then I wanted to come back in case *you* had found her.

I wanted to be here to greet her," she said, shrugging sadly.

Damon nodded. "She's safe," he said shortly.

"Oh, good!" Cora said, her hands flying to her face in relief. She turned her eyes up as if in prayer. "Thank you. And is she . . . "

"We didn't speak to her," I said. "We weren't able to get inside Samuel's house."

"What happened?" Cora asked.

I settled onto the ground and began telling her what we'd found at Samuel's. Occasionally, Damon would chime in with his own observations. Cora nodded, but I could tell all of it—revenge, staking, a beautiful, centuries-old vampire controlling myself and Damon and inspiring Samuel's hatred of us—was beyond her comprehension. It was beyond *anyone's* rational comprehension.

"Ultimately, we've gotten almost nowhere," I said, discouraged.

"Not exactly," Cora said, hopefully. She pulled a paper from her dress pocket and began to unfold it. "I found this in Whitechapel. It's an advertisement for a benefit for the Magdalene Asylum in just a few days. And look what it says at the bottom: 'Hosted by Samuel Mortimer, Vote Samuel for Councilor of London,'" Cora read out loud. "He's throwing another party, giving us another chance to get to Violet."

"The Magdalene Asylum?" I asked, taking the advertisement and reading it for myself. "What is that?"

"It's for unwed mothers and wayward girls," Cora said knowingly.

"Wayward girls?" Damon repeated.

"Yes. And when some girls can't make rent, the Magdalene Asylum will take them in. One of the girls from the Ten Bells had to go when she became pregnant," Cora trailed off. "Jenny went in back in May. She had her baby in August, but we haven't heard anything about either of them since," Cora said.

"Do you think . . . " I paused, wondering at the enormity of what I was going to ask her.

"I think we should find out more about the Asylum, about how Samuel is involved," Cora said. It was true; if we could get closer to Samuel from another angle, maybe we'd have more clues. And more leads to Violet. We'd have to be smarter this time around, not reveal ourselves too soon.

"What if you went to live in the Asylum?" I asked Cora, the beginnings of a plan forming in my mind. It was risky, but it was the only thing I could come up with.

Fear flickered in Cora's eyes. "What do you mean, *live*?"

"Not forever," I said hastily. "Just for a few days, to see what really goes on there. We'd make sure you were protected. I saw the way you performed in the park. If you could do that, they'd never suspect you. And then we could figure out how Samuel is connected."

"It's not a terrible idea," Damon said grudgingly. "But what if Samuel recognizes her?"

I paused briefly. I hadn't considered that. "What if he does recognize her?" I asked, thinking out loud. "He'll think she left the warehouse when he fled London looking for us and ended up on the streets. In his mind, she'd be just another wayward girl. He doesn't know she's with us," I said, hoping it were true.

"A wayward girl?" Cora wrinkled her nose. "My whole life in London, I've been trying to prove that's not who I am."

"You don't have to do it. I was just talking off the top of my head," I offered. Maybe it was asking far too much from her. "I want you to be safe."

Cora shook her head. "Damon's right. It's not a terrible idea. And if it helps save other girls from being compelled . . ." She shivered. "We'll all go tomorrow. You can say you found me in the street by the Ten Bells. I'll put dirt on my face and . . ."

Just then, steam began erupting from the teakettle in the center of the fire.

"I made you tea," Cora said shyly, interrupting herself. "Do you drink tea, or only blood?"

"I'd love some," I said. I wasn't thirsty for tea, at least not the human kind. But despite myself, my heart went out to Cora for trying. She reminded me of Violet, always trying to see the bright side of things and never seeming depressed for long.

Not to be outdone, Damon nodded in agreement. "Is there anything you can't do, Miss Cora? You're our secret weapon," Damon said in an exaggerated Southern drawl.

I smiled. After a moment, Damon sat down next to me. It was a tiny détente, but it was something. I took a sip of tea, and as the hot liquid warmed my blood, I didn't think about feeding.

"You know, Katherine always thought I was a gentleman," Damon mused, glancing at me. "Except during a few choice activities." I stiffened. It was the verbal equivalent of a crack of thunder, a sign that Damon wasn't interested in keeping the peace between us.

"Katherine?" Cora asked, her face registering confusion. "She was the beautiful vampire?"

"It doesn't matter," I said.

"Apparently, she's the reason we're all on the run from Samuel," Damon said at the same time. "She fell in love with me, and Samuel couldn't deal with it."

"Damon, let it go." My impatience was getting the best of me. "It doesn't matter what happened twenty years ago or who loved whom more. Katherine's gone. She can't love *anyone.*" I knew he was looking for a fight, but I wouldn't give him that satisfaction.

"She was *mine,*" he said, seething.

"Really?" Cora's voice cut through the tension. She stepped between us. "That's what you plan to do? Fight each other over some long-dead vampire while a live one is terrorizing the streets, not to mention framing Damon for murder and holding my sister captive?"

"No," Damon said contritely. "I just don't like it when my brother disrespects me. If Stefan minds himself, then we'll be fine."

"Right," I shot back. "And if no one bruises Damon's fragile ego, we'll be best friends."

Cora opened her mouth as if to say something, then closed it. She glanced between the two of us. "Fine. But if you keep fighting, then I'm leaving. And I'm not sure any of us would survive on our own."

Without another word, she swept off into the darkness of the tunnel, leaving Damon and me alone.

The firelight flickered on the dirt wall, making our shadows loom large and ghostly over us.

"Katherine was the one for me," Damon said petulantly, lost in his own world. "Why can't you accept that?"

"She didn't love either of us," I said flatly.

"Maybe she compelled you," Damon said. "But with me . . ."

"Stop it!" I exploded, springing up and shaking his shoulders. I stared into my brother's eyes. The whites were bloodshot, but the irises were dark and huge in the light from the fire, the pupils dilated. I held on to his shoulders even as I sensed Damon's muscles twitching beneath my grasp. But he didn't try to break free.

He raised a dark eyebrow. "Stop what? Stop telling the truth?"

I roughly pushed him away. "Stop bringing up the past," I said, balling up my fists. "It's pointless. Katherine is dead. And you will be, too, if you don't give up this ridiculous vendetta. Cora's right—we need to worry about the vampires that are still alive. We need to save Violet, and then leave London. Can we at least agree on that?"

"Whatever you say, brother," Damon bit back, standing up and stretching his arms over his head. "Now, if you'll excuse me, I'm going to feed."

Once his footsteps had faded, I lay down quietly to sleep.

7

"All in, brother," Damon advised, clapping his hand on my shoulder.

I was back in Mystic Falls, deep in the woods, where we always went in our youth when we were up to no good. We'd tie our horses to a tree and stay up all night, drinking slugs of whiskey, playing cards, and talking about girls. There was a heavy mist over the pine needle–covered ground and a sharp chill in the air. It was fall, and I was fifteen, eager to be a man in any situation.

Surrounding me were the Giffin brothers, Matthew Hartnett, Nathan Layman, and Damon. A few years older, Damon had been skipping out on our gatherings in the woods lately in favor of nights at the Tavern.

"He ain't allowed to have a coach! Stefan's gotta play for himself, or else I ain't interested," Ethan Giffin called, swigging from his flask. With his curly red hair and round face, Ethan reminded me of an overfed toddler.

"I'm not coaching, I'm just giving some brotherly advice. Do you have a problem with that?" Damon challenged.

"Fine," Ethan said, sitting back on the log. His brother, Calvin, glared at us angrily.

"Besides, Stefan doesn't need my advice. He's smarter than me," Damon said, glancing at his own cards. A few crumpled bills were thrown in a pile, along with a belt buckle, a cigarette lighter, and Clementine Haverford's handkerchief. ("Straight from her bosom!" Ethan Giffin had assured us with a cackle.) The winner would take it all—or lose everything.

"All in," I said, throwing a five-dollar bill on the pile. It was my own small fortune.

One by one, everyone displayed their cards. My heart pounded more and more with each reveal. My hand was better than the two jacks that Calvin presented, and better than Nathan's three queens. Finally, I showed my own hand—a straight flush of hearts.

I scooped up my prizes, beaming at Damon in victory.

"Rise and shine!" I was startled awake by the voice. Disoriented, I blinked up at Damon, his outburst from the night before apparently forgotten. Seeing him now, just after he'd appeared in my dream, was surprising. He was so similar in appearance to the brother of my youth and yet such a profoundly different person. Back then, it had been easy. We knew our strengths complemented each other's, and we were generous with our mutual admiration. He was confident and daring, while I was smart and cautious. Now, we viewed each other with suspicion.

The shadow of a beard covered the lower half of his face. I'd never seen Damon with a beard before, but it suited the air of menace he projected.

I had to look twice when Cora appeared. True to her word, she'd taken the preparations for today seriously. She was wearing the tattered, stained dress she'd worn two days prior. Her hair was mussed so it stuck up in odd angles around her face, and she'd rubbed dirt on her cheeks and forehead. She looked the part of a fallen woman. Which was exactly the point.

"All in," I murmured.

"All in?" Damon glanced at me curiously, but I didn't explain and he didn't press. I didn't want him to ruin what was still an untarnished memory.

Once we got aboveground, we turned in the opposite direction of Lansdowne House. According to Cora, the Magdalene Asylum was just on the edge of Whitechapel,

the site of Samuel's Ripper murders. Would anyone recognize Damon? He was wearing his cloak with the hood
pulled far over his forehead. Combined with the beard,
he looked nothing like the dashing, debonair suspect the
newspapers had described. I allowed my shoulders to
relax.

Finally, we reached a decrepit brick building at the far
end of an alleyway. It was enclosed by an iron fence, and
the solid black doors of the entrance looked ominous. It
didn't seem the type of place to save women. Rather, it
looked like a sort of prison: a place where wayward women
could be locked away and forgotten. I glanced at Cora,
worried, but she stared resolutely ahead.

"At least you'll have a roof over your head. More than
we have, at any rate," Damon said, breaking the silence.

I shot an annoyed glance at Damon, but Cora broke out
into nervous giggles. "It is awful, isn't it?" she said. "And
yet, if I had to choose between here, Whitechapel, or the
tunnel, I suppose I'd choose here. At least I know they'll
offer meals that aren't rat's blood or Alfred's horrible Ten
Bells fish special. Don't be too jealous, lads." She flashed a
smile, but I could tell she was uneasy.

I was, too. "I'll come visit every day. We both will,"
I said as I steeled my courage and rapped sharply on the
door. The three of us stood in anticipation as it slowly
creaked open.

An enormously tall man wearing a priest's robe opened the door and stared down at us. A crucifix hung from his neck, swinging back and forth like a pendulum. I averted my eyes. While it was a myth that crucifixes could be used to torment our kind, they never failed to remind me how unholy and evil my past had been.

"Yes, my children?" he asked stiffly. "What brings you to the Magdalene Asylum?"

Damon stepped forward. "I'm Damon de . . . Croix," he said, catching himself just before he introduced himself as Damon DeSangue. "And this is my brother, Stefan. Like everyone in London, we're shocked by the rash of murders in our city and wish to help keep potential victims off the streets. We found this young girl at the Ten Bells Tavern and offered her our help by guiding her here."

"Quite good," the man said, his gaze flicking to Cora, standing on the step below us. She'd crossed her arms over her chest and was rocking back and forth on her heels. I couldn't tell if she was acting or if the stress had simply become too much for her to handle. Whatever the reason, it was effective.

"Come in." The priest ushered us through the heavy black doors, shutting them behind us with a thud. Inside, the entrance had a vaulted ceiling. Directly in front of us, a saint stared out sorrowfully from a stained-glass window. The air smelled like dust and incense and antiseptic. It reminded me of a church, with its many statues and candles.

I could hear pipes clanking, and the shuffle of footsteps. A girl hurried by, her head bowed. She was wearing a gray dress and bonnet and muttering to herself. I watched Cora's eyes follow her. I reached out to squeeze her hand to let her know everything would be all right, but stopped when I noticed the priest's disapproving gaze.

"I'll fetch Sister Benedict to assist you. She'll assess the girl's . . . suitability," the priest said, as he headed up a set of stairs.

"Home sweet home," Cora murmured shakily.

Just then, a small woman in a nun's habit glided down the staircase. Her face was red and wrinkled, and she wore small spectacles over her watery green eyes. She stared at Cora with an inscrutable expression on her pinched face.

"Hello, Sister," Damon said, bowing to her.

The nun swiveled toward Damon. "Good day," she said, a small smile lighting up her wizened face. Typical Damon. He could charm anyone. "I'm Sister Benedict. Please, come with me," she said, nodding to a small annex underneath another stained glass saint. The room was furnished with a desk, a bookshelf, and several chairs.

She sat at the desk and blinked up at us expectantly. "Gentlemen, please sit." As we got settled, Sister

Benedict pulled a well-worn leather Bible from a bookshelf and wordlessly handed it to Cora. Cora took it, curtseyed, and perched on a rickety chair in the far corner of the alcove.

"My brother and I have taken an **interest** in your fine institution," Damon began. "We've been reading the news of the Ripper with horror, and want to protect any vulnerable young ladies we come across. This seems the place to carry out our mission. We believe that there is providence in the fall of a sparrow."

"Yes, thank the Lord," the nun said piously, crossing herself. I glanced sharply at Damon. *Providence in the fall of a sparrow.* That was from *Hamlet.* Since when did Damon quote Shakespeare? But he only half-shrugged at me, as if to say, *You don't know everything about me, brother.*

"We intend to be generous benefactors of the Asylum," Damon said in a low, charismatic voice, holding the nun's gaze with his own. "Would one thousand pounds per annum be suitable?"

Watching Damon use compulsion reminded me of when, as a child, he would turn a magnifying glass on the ants that marched around the porch of Veritas. They'd be minding their own business when all of a sudden, they'd be caught and writhing in Damon's grasp. It was as terrible to watch then as it was now, even though I knew it was necessary.

"One thousand pounds!" Sister Benedict gasped. "Why, that would do so much for our girls. And, of course, for this girl you found, whom we're most eager to assist," she said, shooting a look at Cora, who kept her eyes downcast. "We have much experience reclaiming the souls of the wicked."

"The girl's name is Co . . . Cordelia," I lied. Cordelia had been our maid back in Mystic Falls. She'd been wise and watchful, and I'd always suspected she knew of Katherine's true nature. In many ways, Cora had similar attributes. "And she's not wicked. Not like that. We found her outside a tavern where she worked as a barmaid. She had been thrown out on the street for refusing the tavern owner's advances. "

"Well, I do appreciate two generous, God-fearing men like you taking an interest in her and in our mission. We'll set her on the path to a better way of life. And to thank you for your generous donation, of course you're invited to our benefit at the end of the week."

"A benefit?" Damon asked, leaning toward her. Out of the corner of my eye, I saw a photograph on the wall, underneath a picture of a sorrowful Saint Anthony. The photograph was of Samuel, smiling triumphantly as he cut a ribbon in front of the same heavy black doors.

"Why, yes," Sister Benedict said. "All the girls get to go; it's a very exciting event. Samuel Mortimer arranges it. I'm sure you know of him?" she asked expectantly.

Damon's mouth twisted into a grimace. "I do. Mr. Mortimer is a shining beacon of philanthropy, a truly inspiring man. Unfortunately, our family got into a bit of a messy disagreement years back, and there's still some bad blood between our clans. I'd just as rather be . . . *silent* donors," Damon explained.

"Of course," Sister Benedict said quickly.

"Thank you," Damon said as I pulled at my collar. The room was boiling, and I felt uncomfortable in more ways than one.

"I know you're both busy, so let's get Cordelia taken care of and up on her feet." Sister Benedict snapped her fingers, and immediately I heard the clicking sounds of footsteps on the wood floor. A tall nun, nearly my height and twice my girth, stormed into the room. Her face was long and horselike, with a pointy nose and lips so thin and pale they almost disappeared into her face. She had a few errant black whiskers sticking out from her chin. I recoiled. Nun or not, she was the ugliest woman I'd ever seen.

"Sister Agatha, we have another girl. And she's come to us in the nick of time." Sister Benedict pointed at Cora. "Don't worry, gentlemen. You did well to bring her to us. By the time she's rehabilitated, no one will even recognize her."

"Please take good care of her," I said as Sister Agatha escorted Cora out of the room. The nun glanced at me over her shoulder disdainfully, and I felt my stomach sink. Cora was in for a rough time.

Cora turned to us from the doorway. "Thank you so much, sirs. I hope to one day repay your kindness." She gazed straight at me and smiled sweetly.

I nodded, and she gave me an almost imperceptible wink.

"Sister Agatha will take great care of her," Sister Benedict said haughtily.

"Of course," Damon said soothingly. "My brother sometimes takes the concept of turning the other cheek and being kind to the needy a bit too far. But there are worse vices. To set his mind at ease, and for our own consideration as we allocate funds for the Magdalene Asylum, may we have a tour? We always like to feel invested in the causes we support, and we'd like to make sure young Cordelia is in the place most appropriate to her needs."

I had to hand it to Damon: When it came to getting his way, he was good.

Sister Benedict rose from her chair. "It's normally against policy to allow gentlemen inside. But considering your generosity, as well as your clear commitment to the poor, lost girls of Whitechapel, I suppose I could show you around. But I do have to warn you. The girls are not fully rehabilitated, and seeing a member of the opposite sex sometimes overexcites them."

"Thank you for letting us know," Damon said seriously. "We'll be careful."

"Just don't be alarmed. Follow me," she directed. "Sister Agatha will take Cordelia on her own tour and get her settled. I'm certain you'll feel it's the right place for her," Sister Benedict said as she swept out the door, hardly looking back to see if we were following as she led us deeper into the Asylum.

The more steps we took into the basement, the hotter it became. Damon had been wrong. The tunnel wasn't the closest we could get to hell—the basement of the Magdalene Asylum was.

At the end of the staircase was a single wooden door. Sister Benedict, seemingly unaffected by the temperature, twisted the knob and instantly, I realized why it was so hot. Vast metal tubs full of scalding water crowded the room, each one lined with girls in gray smocks, their sleeves rolled up as they washed pile after pile of soiled linen.

"This is our laundry room, where the girls work. They clean the linens from the Magdalene Sisters of Charity hospital. We find that physical labor prevents idle thoughts. And since idle thoughts lead to evil deeds, they are literally scrubbing their minds clean of sin," she explained proudly, gesturing to the rows of girls bent over scrub boards. Their faces were bright red and shiny with sweat, and none of them acknowledged one another, nor the fact that we were watching and talking about them as though they were animals in a zoo.

Just then, Sister Benedict turned and directed her gaze toward a small, dark-haired girl in the corner. The girl's shoulder blades stuck out from beneath her gray cotton smock like wings.

"Daphne," she barked. The girl turned toward us, blinking in fear. "Idle hands are the devil's tools."

I suddenly regretted our decision to bring Cora here. When she had first told us about the Magdalene Asylum, I'd imagined it to be similar to the rooming houses above the Ten Bells: full of girls who'd fallen on hard times, but who had a roof over their heads and friends to commiserate with. I wasn't expecting it to be some sort of workhouse. Even the tunnel seemed better than this. I wondered if it was too late to free Cora; I didn't want her to have to endure even a day of this torment.

"I'm sorry, Sister!" the girl said as she went back to rubbing a sheet against the board.

"May we see the rest of the facility?" I asked, wanting to spare the girl another moment of Sister Benedict's presence.

"See the rest of the facility?" Sister Benedict repeated, her glasses sliding down her nose. "Well, it wouldn't be appropriate to allow gentlemen into the living quarters, where the girls change and sleep. We do want to protect our charges."

I was tempted to argue, but didn't. Instead, I stared into her watery eyes, concentrating on a single white speck embedded in her left iris. In a young woman, the mark would have been fascinatingly beautiful, but on Sister Benedict it looked sinister.

"I understand that," I said slowly. "But it's nowhere near nightfall. We simply want to see whether we should add an additional donation for the improvement of the facilities. "

Sister Benedict's eyes lit up greedily. "Oh! Well, in that case, I'm sure we can make an exception," she said. "All right. But only briefly," she allowed as she turned on her heel, her long robe sweeping the path we were to follow.

As we walked up the stairs, I heard a far-off shriek. It was a heartwrenching cry, but Sister Benedict didn't seem the least bit perturbed.

"Did you hear that?" I asked Damon softly, but Damon only shrugged.

"How many girls are here?" I asked.

"We usually have fifty or so at a time. And of course, our hope is that they will all be rehabilitated. But some . . . " Sister Benedict shook her head. "Some are too far gone by the time they get to us. Imagine a pigeon getting stuck on a slick of tar. If you got it out right away, brushed off its feathers, and cleaned its feet, it'd be right as rain. But wait too long, and it's stuck. Ruined. We hope to get the girls before that point. And of course, before anything else gets them," she added.

"Such as Jack the Ripper?" I asked.

"Shh!" She turned to me sharply. "We don't speak of him here. We don't want to frighten the girls."

At the top of the stairs, she took an iron key from a ring hidden in the voluminous folds of her robe, and opened a large wooden door.

I blinked. The room was ballroom-sized and lined with fifty identical cots pushed close together. Some were occupied even though it was daytime. I saw a girl at the far end of the room writhing back and forth, as if in terrible pain. Her hands were over her face and she was making low, guttural sounds.

"What happened to her?" Damon asked.

"She has bad dreams, that one. Doesn't talk to anyone. We're waiting for the doctor to come and see what's wrong." Sister Benedict sighed heavily.

Just then, a door at the opposite end of the room opened and Cora shuffled in, followed by Sister Agatha. Cora was dressed in the same floor-length shapeless gray smock all the other girls wore, and her hair was covered by a dingy gray bonnet. Her eyes were wide with fright, and even from across the room I could tell she was no longer acting.

"Well, that was everything. Are you satisfied with our facilities?" Sister Benedict asked.

I stole a glance at Cora, who nodded and tried to look more confident.

"Yes," I said, hoping I wouldn't regret it.

"Good," Sister Benedict's face broke into a smile. "Now, if you'll be so kind as to come back downstairs, we'll discuss the specifics of your donation."

"Please," I said. "Before we depart, I want to say good-bye to Cordelia. I'd like to leave her with some encouraging words, if that's all right, ma'am . . . I mean, Sister," I said, catching myself.

"Of course," Sister Benedict agreed. I crossed the room, grateful that Sister Agatha took the hint and stepped a few paces away. Damon did his part by distracting the nuns with questions about how the Asylum was founded.

"Cora," I said, making sure I stood far enough away that our conversation wouldn't arouse the suspicion of the nuns. I took in her new attire, my gaze landing on her bare neck.

"Where's your charm?" I asked urgently.

"They made me take it off, but I have it in my pocket." She gave me a crooked smile. "Don't worry, I'll be fine. I can handle myself. And these nuns seem harsh, but they're nothing like the ones that taught us at the parish school back in Ireland," she said, trying to assuage my fears.

She was brave, but that didn't mean we needed to be reckless. "If it ever gets to be too much, or too dangerous . . . we can track Samuel another way. We can—"

"I'll be *fine*. We don't have much time now. Meet me across from the gates tomorrow morning at six-thirty sharp. The girls all go to the morning mass at seven. I'll sneak away."

Just then, I heard the insistent sound of rosary beads clicking closer toward me. I whirled around.

"Are you ready?" Sister Agatha asked, arching one of her dark eyebrows. Damon trailed after her.

"Yes," I said.

Damon cleared his throat. "We'll be back soon. And remember, you've already received our first check," Damon said, pinning the nun with his eyes. Sister Benedict nodded once as she escorted us out of the room, down the stairs, and back outside.

"We'll take good care of Cordelia," Sister Benedict said as she closed the door on us. "And of course, the invitation to the benefit is an open one. I know the world of business can be godless, but in good deeds there's always unity. And with such a handsome check, I can't imagine that our benefactor, Mr. Mortimer, wouldn't want to thank you himself."

"I agree, and when the time is right, we'll be delighted to meet with him," Damon said, sarcasm so heavy in his voice I shot a warning glance at him. There was a chill in the air, and the sky was filled with large black rain clouds. A few drops spattered against my coat. I glanced up, trying to gauge when the clouds would break.

All I could hope was that the storm wasn't a warning of things to come.

8

$\mathfrak{I}$ glanced back at the imposing door of the Magdalene Asylum, wondering if Cora was being put straight to work in the laundry or whether our fake generosity would inspire leniency. For Cora's sake, I hoped so.

"Let's have a drink. A tumbler of whiskey might calm your nerves," Damon suggested as soon as we turned the corner.

I considered the offer. I was hungry, and whiskey often worked well to quench a craving. But whiskey had a less predictable effect on Damon. Sometimes, he could drink it and seem relaxed, as though he didn't have a care in the world. Other times, he'd drink it and seem edgy and violent. I decided to take my chances.

"That'd be nice," I said.

Damon nodded as he turned away from Whitechapel. "You know, brother, there was a time I thought we'd never speak civilly to each other again. But now look at us. You've changed."

What about last night? I wanted to ask. I didn't. It was funny the way that just the mention of Katherine's name could unhinge him, even after all these years. But if he wasn't bringing up her name now, I certainly wouldn't either. Instead, I indulged in his belief that we were getting along exceptionally well. Maybe the more I tried to believe it, the more it would be true.

"I haven't changed. Unless you're finally seeing the man I really am," I said. I'd spent the past two decades trying to return to the human I'd been before Katherine had entered my life. But Damon was the one who seemed different. Still impulsive, still possessive of Katherine's memory, and still brooding, but also a little bit more . . . human.

"Whatever you say," Damon said, smiling. "Maybe it's just that middle age suits you. It was always how you acted," he teased as we headed toward the glittering Thames. It was funny how familiar I had gotten with every city in which I had lived. Was it simply because cities, like humans, no longer surprised me? Of course there were different customs and residents and accents, but every city had its dark history, its hidden secrets.

"I wonder whether Samuel has killed anyone today,"

Damon said, nodding at an elderly man carrying a sack of newspapers on his back.

"Hasn't he already killed enough?" I asked dully as Damon compelled the man into giving him a paper. "I'm not sure I want to know."

"I do," Damon said, folding the newspaper under one arm. "Samuel thinks he's so clever, but we know all of his moves now. And that's encouraging. My guess is that we'll kill him and his brat of a brother before the week's out. And then, brother, the city is ours. Or"—Damon scratched his head, as though he were deep in thought—"the city will be mine. And maybe, if you don't annoy me, I'll let you live here, too."

We'd reached Fleet Street, just a few miles down from our tunnel, and the streets were bustling with late-afternoon foot traffic. Now was not the time to talk about Samuel.

"It's not that easy, Damon," I said, but I knew my words would fall on deaf ears. All I wanted was whiskey and a chance to forget what I'd seen that morning, even if only for a few hours.

"Haven't you learned by now?" Damon asked, glancing sharply at me. "Nothing's easy." He quickly turned a corner into an alley, then ducked through a low entranceway. The bar inside was narrow and dark and smelled of sawdust and spilled ale. I relaxed. No one would find us here.

"Nothing like having a drink and discussing old times," Damon said as he made his way to the back of the bar. There sat two sunken club chairs, secluded from the other patrons. "It's like we're back at the Mystic Falls Tavern— all that's missing is a sultry vampire and some Confederate soldiers."

"I don't think anything could be like old times, brother," I said, reflexively looking behind me to see if we'd been followed. But no one seemed concerned with anything but their drinks. Most of the patrons were sitting alone at tables, some writing in ledger pads, others staring off into the distance. The pub was clearly one where people liked to go when they wanted to be alone.

"Whatever you say," Damon said, sinking into a cracked leather chair and propping his feet up on a low-slung table. He pulled out the paper and flipped immediately to the society pages. "So if nothing's like old times, then maybe it's your turn to get me a drink."

Of course Damon always found a way to twist my words to his benefit.

The barman was elderly and had a close-cut white beard. He was wearing a filthy apron splattered with drink stains. I wished we could switch lives. I'd gladly spend the rest of eternity serving drinks to men whose biggest sin was downing too many pints of beer, not pints of blood.

"Two whiskeys. Charge to Sir Stefan Pine," I said,

waiting for the sensation when my mind melded with his.

But this time, something was wrong. It felt like the compulsion was hanging in the air between us, suspended and unclaimed. And that's when I realized the barman was paying no attention to me. Instead, he was looking over my shoulder, at Damon, still reclining in the leather club chair. His ankle was crossed over his knee, his hair was flopping over his eyes, and his tie was undone.

"Two whiskeys?" I prodded nervously. Damon was flipping through a newspaper, oblivious to my presence. But the barman didn't turn, and I realized with horror that he wasn't the only one focused on Damon. Two men had left off playing cards in the corner and directed their stares at my brother. They were glancing at a spot above the barman's head, then back to Damon. I followed their gaze and saw what had arrested their attention. A broadsheet from the newspaper was affixed to the wall, just beside a shelf of dusty liquor bottles.

JACK THE RIPPER! NO ONE IS SAFE!

What was underneath the words caused my chest to seize in fear: a drawing of Damon. This time, the likeness between the image and Damon was undeniable.

"Damon!" I hissed under my breath. "Run. They've recognized you." I wouldn't risk looking at him, lest suspicion fall on me, too. I focused on the pitted surface of the bar, as though I was patiently waiting for my whiskeys.

I heard a commotion behind me and whirled around. Damon had shot up and was racing out of the bar at vampire speed, his tie falling to the floor as he ran. I watched him dash past me. I knew it was a risk to be associated with Damon, but I had to follow, to do what I could to protect him in the maze of London streets. I bolted after him.

"*Jack the Ripper!*"

"*Call the police!*"

I heard the cacophony of voices behind us, each desperate yell spurring me to run harder and faster, blindly following Damon through the rain-soaked streets. The wide cobblestone thoroughfare of Fleet Street was crammed with carriages going in both directions. Following Damon's lead, we took our chances dodging through the chaotic London traffic. Our footsteps thwacked against wet ground and blood rushed in my ears. I forgot about my hunger—all I cared about was Damon and me making it back to the tunnel.

"Go, go, go!" I urged, although I couldn't tell whether I was speaking to Damon or myself.

"*Stop them!*"

"*Police!*" There was now a crowd on our tail, and coachmen were jumping down from their carriages to join the fray. Behind us, I heard a lone shot, followed by glass shattering. And then, a figure leapt in front of me.

I found myself face-to-face with a wild-eyed drunk.

He was dressed in rags, and his breath smelled stale and rancid.

"Got him!" he yelled, clamping his hand around my arm. I reflexively jerked my arm back, slamming the man's body against the glass window of a storefront. The impact broke the glass behind him, and when the scent of blood filled the air, I knew he'd been cut.

"That's not the Ripper!" another man yelled, running up to me. I stayed still, hoping Damon was far enough away. More and more men were approaching, brandishing knives and broken bottles.

"He was with him in the tavern!" I heard a voice shout from the back of the crowd, but it was far too late. In the commotion, I broke free, using my vampire speed to catch up to Damon, and the mob of fifty that was hot on Damon's trail. In the far distance, I heard the ringing of police bells.

I didn't dare look behind me. It was as if my brother and I were back in the pasture at Veritas, racing against each other to get to the stables. Only now, we weren't running for personal bragging rights. We were running for our lives.

We pushed ourselves, giving an extra burst of speed until the noise of the mob faded behind us. Finally, we reached the tunnel and jumped down. The air smelled dank, and drops of water oozed from the walls like blood from a wound. Still, I was relieved to be there.

Damon and I stared at each other, panting hard.

"Well, at least I worked up an appetite," Damon said dully. He rose to his feet, and I could tell he was trying to hide the fact that he was still winded, sweat running down his face. "I'm going to find some food. Don't wait for me."

"Fine," I said, still catching my breath.

A few minutes later, I heard a moan as Damon undoubtedly sunk his teeth into a nameless tunnel dweller. I felt my own stomach growl in protest as I turned my face to the wall and listened for the scrabble of a rat to at least quell my hunger. But there was nothing.

9

The next morning, I awoke early. Or perhaps I hadn't fallen asleep. All I could think of was Cora, alone in the cold, unfriendly Asylum. But whenever I closed my eyes to conjure her face in my mind—her proud eyes and the spray of freckles on her nose—all I could imagine was Katherine.

In my vision, Katherine was smiling at me, her hair plaited in a long braid tossed over one bare shoulder.

"Can't you smile, Stefan?" she asked, shaking her head at my morose condition.

I tossed and turned. I wanted to forget about Katherine. But it was impossible when I was with Damon. Faint light was coming through the opening to the tunnel. Without waking Damon, I scrambled up the ladder and into the early morning. It was wet and cold and the fog made the Thames difficult to see even from a few paces away.

I hurried to the Magdalene Asylum, hands jammed in my pockets, shuffling my feet and singing an ill-mannered drinking song that often broke out at pubs. I wanted anyone who saw me to assume I was just a drunk and leave me alone. Rain was falling softly from the dove-gray sky, and the cobblestones were slick.

Midway to the Asylum, I spotted a bakery with a red awning. It was the shop where Cora and I had gone before the park, what seemed like a lifetime ago.

On a whim, I entered.

"Six buns, please," I said, holding the baker's gaze until she nodded and brought me a white sack.

"Thank you," I said, noticing the poster behind the counter. My stomach sank. Damon's face was everywhere.

The woman followed my gaze. "He's back in London," she explained. "Nobody's safe." She squinted harder at me, and I took that as my cue to hurry away. The family resemblance between Damon and me was faint, but it was there, as indelible as ink. I couldn't risk someone associating me with my brother, especially since we'd been spotted together at the tavern last night.

Treats in hand, I settled on an ivy-covered bench across the street from the Asylum. I pulled out my watch. Twenty minutes after six.

As expected, a side door opened a few minutes later, and two lines of girls filed out, as though they were soldiers on the march. There were about fifty in all, identically clad in gray smocks, their hair pulled back and covered by bonnets. Some of the girls looked no older than thirteen, while others seemed to be in their late twenties. I had to squint to tell them apart. It would be difficult to find Cora.

"Order!" Sister Benedict barked at the front of the line. "Now, think of the prayers you'll offer to God!" She marched them through the gates and onto the street.

"Cora!" I hissed, disguising it as a cough. "Cora!"

I saw movement from the far line, and then Cora turned toward me and gave a quick smile. As the group turned a corner, she stole away.

"You made it," Cora whispered, her back pressed against the sandstone building as she inched farther down the street and toward a tiny cobblestone-paved alley.

"Of course. I was worried about you. Are you all right?" I asked, following her lead and trying to shield her with my body. In the distance, the church bells pealed.

"Thankfully, yes," Cora said urgently. "But other girls weren't so lucky. I saw something last night," she continued, sinking to sit on a concrete step. Here, in the alley, we were partially covered from the rain by the stone overhang of an abandoned building.

"What?" I asked, my imagination running wild, the bakery bag in my lap all but forgotten.

"Samuel and Henry came to the Asylum in the middle of the night."

"What? Why?" I asked.

"They're drinking from the girls. I saw it with my own eyes. It was terrible. You have to stop it." Silence hung in the air between us. I was afraid to stir. In the distance, a crow cawed and a police bell rang, all reminders that we were not alone.

"It took me ages to fall asleep last night, but I eventually nodded off," Cora said, glancing up at the sky. "The next thing I knew, I was startled awake by a noise. I saw Samuel and Henry walk into the room. As soon as I saw them, I pulled my sheet over my head and lay on my side, pretending to be asleep, but the sheets are so thin that I still saw everything," Cora said breathlessly. "They stopped by a few beds, silently waking the girls. One of them was Winnie, who was sleeping to the right of me. I stayed as rigid as I could and was just clutching my charm. Oh, Stefan, at one point, they were so close I felt Henry's hand brush against my forehead. I heard Samuel say, 'Fresh blood,' and I almost stopped breathing, I was so frightened. But then they moved on to another girl. He didn't recognize me, I'm sure of it," she added with conviction.

"How many girls did they take?" I asked. I imagined

Samuel, debonair and fresh from a night out. He'd be wearing cologne and a tux, with his hair slicked back and his necklace tucked underneath his starched white shirt. I imagined him and Henry stealing into the girls' dormitory and choosing the ones they were to feast on as if they were pastries at a buffet. I imagined the girls—sleepy and terrified, heavy-footed under the veil of compulsion, following them down the rickety stairs to the laundry and offering their necks, feeling pain radiate through their bodies as Henry and Samuel drank their fill. I shuddered.

"Five. Maybe six. It was hard to tell." Cora masked her face with her hands, as if even remembering the scene was far too much for her to bear. "They took Winnie and Evelyn, and Louise, and I think they took a little girl named Clare as well. She was Irish, so of course I was hoping to look out for her . . ." Cora trailed off. When she spoke next, it was in a tiny voice: "I followed them."

"You did?" I asked, impressed.

Cora nodded. "I tried to be so quiet. I know how you and Damon hear things that normal humans don't. I've noticed it," she said, smiling to herself. "I notice *a lot* of things," she added. "But they never looked back. They brought the girls down to a room next to the laundry. There are a lot of rooms down there, a long hallway of doors. I'm not sure where they lead."

I nodded, encouraging Cora to continue her story.

I could feel the anticipation; we were onto something here, getting closer to Samuel. Despite the horrors she was describing, I was excited.

"They took the girls into one of the rooms, what looked like an office, and they started feeding. But it wasn't like the time you ate that rat. That seemed all right. This . . . they'd sink their teeth deep into the girl's neck. I could see blood drip down their backs as they drank. At first I almost screamed. But then . . ."

"What?" I asked. I laced my fingers in hers and gave her hand a small squeeze. It was so small and fragile, and made me feel as if I were holding a baby sparrow.

"Samuel would lean down and whisper to them. Almost as if he were being sweet on them. But Henry . . ." Her face hardened. "Henry had no mercy. Would say that screaming wouldn't do anything, and this was all they deserved. That no one would care if they died and he was doing them a favor. It was terrible to watch. Because all I could think was, what if he was had been doing that to my sister?"

"He's not. Violet's a vampire. She can look out for herself now." It was cold comfort, but it was something.

Cora nodded. "I know. But I couldn't watch anymore. I thought, it would be just my luck, and so stupid, if I were to get caught. I'd be no use to Violet after that."

I squeezed her hand again. That was the problem we

all faced: We were in this together. And although death might be easier, we needed to survive, for each other.

"This morning, the girls were back in their beds. I tried to talk to Clare at breakfast, but Sister Benedict yelled at me. She rapped my fingers. I hadn't gotten that type of punishment since school," Cora said wryly. She loosened my grasp and showed me the back of her hand. Indeed, a faint bluish bruise was spreading across the white skin. I winced.

"It's all right," Cora said. "I've learned my lesson. We're supposed to devote breakfast to silent prayer. And it's not that bad. Some of the girls are nice. There's one, Elizabeth, who used to work at a tavern even worse than the Ten Bells. And Cathy's been kind enough to show me around. I'll be all right, Stefan," Cora said.

I wanted so badly to believe her. No, I *needed* to believe her. I thought of Samuel, his ratlike face buried deep in the neck of one of these girls, and felt my stomach twist with a sense of renewed hatred. He would pay for his actions. He had to.

Cora reached up to tuck her hair behind her ears. In that gesture, I noticed the chain of her vervain charm move, hidden beneath her dress. And suddenly, the kernel of a plan began to form in my mind.

"So you all eat breakfast at the same time?" I asked.

"Oh yes," Cora said. "Sister Benedict makes us. We

have fifteen minutes for meals, in between prayers and work."

In the distance, the chapel bell began to chime. *One, two . . .*

"I should . . ." Cora said, her eyes flicking to the church in concern. The service would be getting out soon, and Cora needed to rejoin the line of the girls back without anyone realizing she'd been missing.

"I brought this for you," I said, holding out the still-warm bag of pastries.

"Oh, *Stefan*!" Cora said, her face breaking into a wide smile. She was so pleased at such a small gesture that I felt ashamed I hadn't done more. She deserved gold and diamonds for what she was doing. And instead, she was exclaiming over a bit of bread as though it were the greatest of treasures. Once we vanquished Samuel, I'd get her anything her heart desired. That was a promise.

"Would you like one?" she said, offering the bag to me.

I picked one out and took a small bite. The bread stuck to the roof of my mouth like glue, tasteless. I had no enjoyment for human food, but I wanted to have a small moment of normalcy with Cora.

"*Mmm*," Cora said contentedly. "They feed us gruel. This is good. Thanks for thinking of me."

"Of course," I said. Then, hesitantly: "You're all I've been thinking of." In a different world, the sentence would have been a precursor to a declaration of love. Instead, I hurried on. "Listen, I have a plan. You know your necklace?"

"Of course," Cora said, reaching into her smock and pulling it out. It glinted in the sun: a tiny ray of hope amid a swirl of darkness.

"The vervain works in a few ways. First, it makes it impossible for vampires to compel you, but it does more than that. It's poisonous and burns us. Even touching the charm is hard for me." The pealing of the bells stopped, and I knew I had only minutes to refine my idea.

"But the worst is when vervain catches a vampire unawares. When I was a human, my father dosed me with vervain. I didn't know. I was in love with a girl . . ."

"Katherine?" Cora asked pointedly.

"Yes," I said. Cora certainly did notice everything. "And Katherine was a vampire. My father was suspicious of her, so he decided to create a test. He slipped vervain into my drink. And as soon as Katherine sank her teeth into me, she sprang back in agony. She was writhing on the floor and foaming at the mouth. And then . . ."

"He knew," Cora said simply.

"Yes. And so did everyone else. But what's important was her reaction. She was in agony. Vervain is like poison— it renders us helpless. So if we could only dose some of the girls with vervain, and wait for Samuel to drink, then . . ."

"You and Damon will be able to attack," Cora said quietly, twisting the necklace back and forth in her fingers. In the distance, I could hear Sister Benedict's voice.

"No talking!" she was saying. "Contemplate what you learned in church."

"You need to go. Damon and I will find more vervain and come up with a way for you to distribute it. Same time tomorrow?" I asked.

Cora nodded, clutching at the charm.

"Good. Stay safe. And know that I'm thinking about you," I said, brushing my lips gently against her cheek. Her skin felt ice cold.

"Good-bye!" Cora said, rushing toward the street so she could slip back in line. She had a high flush in her cheeks, and I knew our plan had galvanized her. And it would work. It had to. After all, if it had worked against Katherine, then it would certainly work on such a bloodthirsty duo as Henry and Samuel.

I stood up and stretched. The rain showed no signs of relenting, but the gloomy weather no longer matched my mood. Instead, I felt alive and ready to take on anyone. And that included vampires.

I practically flew back to the tunnel, knocking into pedestrians and coachmen along the way. At one point I stopped, catching sight of a broadsheet posted outside a bank.

CRIMINAL MOST FOUL! proclaimed the headline above the now-familiar etching of Damon's face. Soon, these posters would come down and Damon would be able to roam the streets of London as a free man. But for now, I was worried about him leaving the tunnel even for a moment.

"Bloody awful, don't you think?" I turned to find a man standing next to me, staring at the broadsheet.

"I suppose so," I said stiffly.

"Won't be for long. We've got all of London looking for him. Thinks he's a fancy man about town, but then gets his jollies from ripping apart them girls. Terrible."

"I suppose no one is ever really what they seem," I said uncomfortably. "If you'll excuse me." I backed away, picking up my pace until I lost sight of him.

I reached the tunnel and climbed down the ladder into the darkness. "Damon!" I called, not bothering to be cautious.

"Good day, brother," Damon said, nodding at me from his perch on the ledge. He was playing a game of solitaire, slapping each card down violently. I knew he was angry about being stuck belowground. But that wasn't my problem. I was sick of tiptoeing around Damon's moods.

"I saw Cora," I said.

"Oh? And how is she?" he asked politely, as though he were inquiring about a long-lost cousin.

"They're using them for blood. Samuel and Henry are feeding on the girls," I said. I swung myself onto the ledge so I was sitting next to my brother.

"Really?" Damon's eyes widened. "That's their blood supply. That's brilliant," he said.

"It's awful!" I retorted.

"Right. Of course it is. But just think. No hunting, and so many girls available that they don't feed enough to kill them. I hate to say it, but Samuel knows what he's doing," Damon said grudgingly. "If they weren't trying to kill me, I would probably join them."

I grimaced. I knew Damon wasn't saying it to shock me—he actually would have.

"I think I have a plan to catch them," I said quietly, almost afraid to voice the idea. I knew it *could* work. But I didn't want to see Damon's sneer or listen to him list all the reasons the plan wouldn't work, all the ways it could go wrong.

"Really? Does it involve you sacrificing yourself? Now that's a plan I could get behind," Damon quipped.

"Vervain," I said simply. "Cora can sneak some in, and she'll dose the girls at breakfast. Then, when Samuel feeds, he'll be poisoned, and we'll be able to attack."

"Vervain," Damon repeated thoughtfully. "That's not bad, brother."

"It grows everywhere back home. But here . . ." I remembered how hard it had been to try to cultivate vervain in the limestone-rich English soil. It wasn't something that grew naturally. I'd nurtured a tiny patch on the grounds of Abbott Manor, but it had required near constant diligence. Back in the States, it had been awful to walk through a field only to suddenly feel dozens of stings around my ankles. The vervain I gave to Violet, which Cora now wore, was from San Francisco—crumbly and dried, like a pressed flower.

"We don't need to grow it. Brother, you need to stop thinking like a farmer. We're in London, where money can get you anything. We can still find it," Damon said mysteriously.

"Where?" I asked.

"Wherever there's a city of vampires, there are anti-dotes. Do you think the war between us and Samuel is the only one brewing in our world?" Damon asked with a twisted grin. "Come. We're going to the Emporium," Damon said. He pulled on a hat to disguise his face. Now that his angular cheekbones, shock of dark hair, and piercing eyes were covered, he didn't look like the man on the broadsheet. He looked like just another Londoner shielding himself from the rain.

Without saying a word, I followed him.

Soon, I realized there were parts of London far worse than Whitechapel. Whitechapel had reminded me of some of the slums of New York City, communities we'd only passed through in a coach. But these areas were even more decrepit. Stray cats yowled in the alleyways, and boarded-up windows faced the streets below. It was impossible to tell whether any of the homes were inhab-ited. I hoped not.

"How do you know this part of town?" I asked. It was nothing like the elegant blocks Damon usually frequented.

"Unfortunately, I lived in this hellhole," Damon said,

grimacing. "You're not the only one who's had to slum it, brother."

"You lived here?" I repeated in disbelief, picking my way over a pile of garbage and broken crates.

"You do what you have to do. Obviously, I prefer feather beds and champagne, but those aren't always available. Besides, the darkness suits me. No one looks at you, no one cares if people go missing. It's real life, brother," Damon continued as we walked down the winding alleyway. The passage was so narrow that only one person could fit at a time.

"When did you arrive in London, anyway?" I asked. I realized I had no idea what Damon had done for the past twenty years. Of course, he had no idea what I'd done either, but I didn't think he was particularly interested. Those twenty years had passed like a summer. Lexi and I had toured the country; we'd had long conversations and had occasionally taken odd jobs to pad our pockets. What had Damon seen?

"I've been here for a while. I knew the States couldn't contain me. I had to seek adventure elsewhere," Damon said cryptically. He stopped in front of the door of a house similar to all the other derelict residences on the streets.

He raised his fist and rapped three times.

"Who's there?" A low, croaky voice called from the other side.

"Damon DeSangue," Damon said in a flawless Italian accent.

The door creaked open and a tiny, wizened man stepped out. He was missing an eye, and the other was oozing a milky white substance. It was difficult to tell his age, or if he was even human.

"James!" Damon said warmly, reaching down to shake his hand.

"Damon! You've been gone far too long. I trust you're not getting into trouble?" James asked, raising the white tufted eyebrow above his sightless eye socket. Suddenly, his remaining eye landed on me. "Who's this?" he asked suspiciously.

"This is Stefan," Damon said. "My brother. Also a vampire. Stefan, this is James, a friend to England's creatures of the night."

"Or anyone who pays," James said, looking me up and down until his eyes finally settled on my lapis lazuli ring. He grinned wryly. "So what can I do for you boys? We have rhinoceros blood. It's a treat for the discerning palate. And can I get you two a cup of goat's blood tea?" he asked, hustling us inside the tiny, cluttered front room.

I startled when I heard mention of goat's blood tea. Most vampires didn't drink anything but human blood, and I'd thought goat's blood was a delicacy only Lexi enjoyed. I wondered who James's other customers were.

The thought drifted away as I stepped farther inside. I blinked in amazement at our surroundings. I'd thought I'd seen it all, or at least heard about things from Lexi. But now I realized there was so much I still had to learn. Frogs packed in jars were lined up against one wall. On another, purplish-red hearts pulsed, suspended in a filmy substance. And an entire shelf was crammed with bowls full of gemstones. Was this where Katherine had gotten the rings?

"You know, Damon, the offer still stands. I'll be willing to put up a very pretty penny for that ring. I've had several inquiries. I know only the owner can benefit from its properties, but several of my kind would like to study it," James said greedily.

"No, this has a certain . . . sentimental value attached to it." Damon shook his head and pulled his arm inside his cloak. "And tea won't be necessary for me. I'm still enjoying human blood. What I'm here for is vervain—a lot of it."

"Vervain." James smiled as he climbed on a stepstool and pulled down a few jars of the lilaclike flowers. "I don't often get vampires looking for vervain. Witches, yes. But vampires tend to avoid the substances that harm them."

Damon smiled tightly as James arranged the jars on the counter. I winced just looking at it.

"So, this will be . . . twenty pounds," James said, pulling a number from thin air.

I pulled off my cuff links in frustration, hoping he would accept them in lieu of twenty pounds in hard cash. I doubted it. Twenty pounds was an astronomical sum. And it wasn't as if we could compel James; running this shop, he'd obviously taken great lengths to protect himself. I could sense an impervious air around him.

"Sure," Damon said smoothly, pulling a fistful of coins from deep within his pockets.

I blinked in amazement. In the flickering candlelight, the golds and silvers blurred together. The coins were round, square, and octagonal, and looked like they came from all over the globe. Where had he amassed such a fortune? And why hadn't he offered it up before now, forcing me to rely on compulsion to get us everything from clothing to cakes?

James's eyes glinted greedily. "Why, thank you, Damon. Of course, we welcome various currencies, but if you're going to be paying in anything that's not sterling, there is a . . . processing fee."

"Take it," Damon said cavalierly, pushing the mountain of coins across the dirty counter.

James took a heavy-looking square coin and squinted at it, causing more liquid to ooze from his eye. "Africa, eh? You don't see many from there. How was it?"

"Hot," Damon said shortly, obviously not interested in having a conversation.

Africa? I blinked at my brother. He was definitely unpredictable.

"Well, here's enough vervain to take down an army of vampires. Although don't outright kill 'em—it'd be bad for business!" James said, laughing and pounding the counter at the hilarity of his joke.

"Thank you," Damon said, watching impassively as James put the jars of vervain into a large burlap sack.

"Now, can I help you with anything else? I have the blood of a Bengal tiger. It's supposed to help with strength and temperament!" James said hopefully, his gaze flicking between me and Damon.

My stomach grumbled. I needed to find a pigeon or a squirrel before my hunger got any worse. Or, I could take the drink James was offering. "All right," I said. Let Damon pay for it. He could certainly afford it.

"Two glasses?" James asked, glancing at Damon.

"No. Tiger blood isn't in my diet," Damon said disdainfully as James passed me a tin cup filled with a liquid as black as coffee. I took a small sip. The blood was rich and buttery tasting. After two decades of drinking watery blood from rabbits, this was heaven. I drained the glass, enjoying the warmth of the meal coursing through my veins.

James smiled. "Glad you enjoyed that. And there's more where that came from."

"Here you go," Damon said, flipping a hexagonal coin onto the counter as payment for my drink.

We bid James good-bye and walked out of the store. I blinked at the sunlight, wondering whether there were more stores like that, hidden all around the world. My mind drifted back to Mystic Falls. A mother-daughter vampire pair had run the apothecary in town, but no one had known they were vampires at the time, and they'd only sold cures for human ailments: herbs for headaches, poultices for wounds. Somehow, I couldn't imagine them having jars of live hearts pumping in their back rooms. But maybe they did.

"It's always good to have friends of various talents, don't you agree, brother? Although I could have bought an elephant for that amount of money. I was tempted to, once, back in India. But then what would I have done with it?" Damon asked, as we walked through the deserted streets. Damon led us in the direction of St. James Park. We walked in silence. I was enjoying the sunshine, while Damon still had to remain cloaked. To outsiders, we were just two men, perhaps playing hooky from work. And for once, I desperately wanted to believe the ruse. Sadly, that would never be the case.

11

The next morning, I hurried across town to Whitechapel, eager to deliver the vervain to Cora. Damon and I had spent the night pressing the flowers into liquid, braving the angry red rashes it left all over our hands and arms. Even now, safely packed in glass vials, the scent made my skin tingle and my eyes burn. Our interactions had been similarly prickly. I'd avoided any mention of Katherine, but Damon had seemed on edge and tried to disguise it by discussing his many conquests. After a while, I'd stopped listening. The story was always the same: beautiful woman, delicious blood, being invited to the finest parties in the area before getting bored and moving on. He didn't yearn for a home the way I did. And more and more, I wondered whether that was a blessing.

I made a hasty stop at the bakery, then hurried to the alley where we'd met before. Cora was already there, hugging her knees to her chest.

"Cora!" I called to her. Her face broke into a forced smile.

"Stefan! I'm glad you're here. Do you have the vervain?" Cora asked.

I held up the vials in response.

"Good," she said, relieved. "They came again last night. This time they took Cathy and Elizabeth. They're my friends, and . . ." She shook her head. "We have to stop them." Cora's lower lip trembled. It was the first time I'd seen her acting anything other than strong, and it caught me off guard.

"Don't worry. Damon and I came up with a plan." I handed her the vials. The glass glinted in the sunlight. "I need you to put some in every girl's drink before the benefit tonight. It only needs to be a drop. Can you do that?"

Cora nodded solemnly.

"It will be fine," I assured her, standing up and planting a kiss on the top of her head as I put the bag of treats next to her. "I'll see you tonight. This will all be over soon," I promised.

"I hope so," Cora said.

"It *will* be," I repeated. "You just have to believe it will."

Cora gave me a soft smile in return, but I could tell her mind was spinning in her own, private way.

"I should get going," I said, standing up and leaving her to her thoughts. Before I continued down the alley, I gave her shoulder a light squeeze. Somehow, I would make sure she was okay.

That night, a brilliant golden-orange sunset lit up the September sky, usually so thick with clouds. It was a beautiful evening, and along the Thames artists were sketching, lovers were walking hand in hand, and buskers were playing instruments and prodding visitors to give them money.

Damon and I blended into the crowd. We were dressed in black, monk robes that I'd procured from a local church. I hadn't even bothered to compel—instead, I'd stolen them outright. It didn't matter. It wasn't as if I was in God's good graces in the first place.

The Magdalene Asylum benefit was being held in the Lanesborough Hotel, opposite Hyde Park. Damon assured me he'd been to dozens of balls there. I couldn't understand why he'd bother. Didn't he tire of them? I'd only been to a few, but had found them all to be the same: too much champagne, too much perfume, too much dancing, and too much talking, none of it about anything of conse-quence. Of course, my solitary walks and endless thinking weren't much better.

"The monk's attire suits you. It's too bad you are a creature of the night, or you might have had quite a career as a man of the cloth," Damon said, taking in my dark robes.

"I already have a guilty conscience. I doubt I could lis-ten to other people's sins," I said, swatting at his arm. But the move was more of a brotherly punch than the start of one of our former brutal fights.

"No drinking, no swearing, no overindulging, no kill-ing . . . face it, you already live a monk's life, brother. Aren't you glad I saved you from the boredom?"

"No," I shook my head. "Aren't you glad I came to shake some sense into you?"

Damon paused, as if pretending to think it over. "No," he said finally. "Sense and I don't mix. You know that."

"What do you think you'll do after this?" I asked, as we turned onto the winding gravel path into the park.

"I don't know," Damon said, a faraway look in his eyes. "What do you do when you've been everywhere? You have to keep things exciting. Maybe someday they'll invent a machine to bring me to another planet."

"I'm serious," I said. "Do you think you could create a life here?" I wanted something substantial, something that would allow me to know my brother as more than the monster he'd become in my mind.

"I don't think I need to *create* my life. I live my life. That's what you need to do, brother," Damon said. I shrugged off his minimalist philosophy—it was devoid of moral structure, but I didn't have time to argue it.

The entrance was lit up by large torches. Well-dressed servants lined the path, and coaches streamed down the cobblestone streets. The Magdalene Asylum seemed to be the most popular cause to support in London these days, and if we hadn't been disguised as monks, our invitations would have been scrutinized closely. As it were, we were ushered through the large glass doors and into a vast ballroom without a backward glance. No one wanted to offend the Church, and everyone assumed we were simply there to offer support and prayers to the Asylum girls the benefit was allegedly honoring.

The walls and roof were all glass and reflected the whirling dancers already on the ballroom floor. Garlands of flowers wrapped around the columns dotting the perimeter of the room, and servers were circulating among the guests, their arms laden with platters of food. Scattered throughout the party in their familiar-looking gray smocks were the girls of the Magdalene Asylum. They were obviously there to remind patrons where all their money was going, but people were gawking at them

as though they were performers at a circus. Most, how-
ever, were huddled in corners in groups, fearfully looking at the attendees as though they might bite. Which
they might.

I squinted, trying to pick Cora out of the crowd. Finally,
I saw her. She was engaged in a low, whispered conversation with a slight girl whose dark hair hung in two plaits
down her back.

"There she is." I elbowed Damon, and together, we
made our way over to her, passing directly in the path of
Sister Benedict's hawklike stare. She waved us on without
glancing at our faces.

"Cora!" I whispered. Cora glanced over, her expression instantly changing from confusion to recognition. She
picked her way through the girls, who all began whispering
among each other, wondering why she was the one chosen
to have an audience with two monks.

"Why, hello, Brother. Don't worry, I said my prayers
yesterday," she said, winking.

I smiled as I leaned in toward her, so my mouth was
only inches from her ear. "You gave some to every girl?" I
asked.

Just then, I felt a tap on my shoulder. I whirled around
and found myself eye to eye with Sister Benedict.

"Hello, Brother," Sister Benedict said, her voice dripping with piety. "How are you finding the evening?"

"Bless you, Sister." I bowed deeply, not giving her a chance to notice I shared a remarkable resemblance to one of the generous de Croix brothers. "The evening is a joy. I'd love to pay my respects to the organizer of tonight's event. When will he be arriving?" I asked, hoping my anticipation wasn't too evident in my question.

Sister Benedict's face broke into a crooked smile. "When you ask, God provides. Look!" She gestured toward a balcony that overlooked the ballroom floor, lit by a bright gas lamp. A man I didn't recognize stepped toward the balcony's railing and looked down. The band stopped playing, and the man spread his arms wide as if in greeting.

"Welcome, friends, to the Magdalene Asylum Benefit Ball!" he said to a roar of applause and a few whistles. "And now for your host, Samuel Mortimer!"

I looked up along with the rest of the crowd as Samuel burst through the doors and onto the balcony to the roar of applause. His blond hair was slicked back behind his ears and curled right above his collar, making him look more lionlike than ever. And on his arm, with her face pale and her long hair piled on top of her head, was Violet. If possible, her eyes looked larger, and her mouth more red, although from this distance it was impossible to tell if it was makeup, a trick of the light, or a smudge of blood from her last feeding. Samuel stood close to her, but it didn't look like she was being held against her will. If anything, whenever Samuel shifted away from her, she would pull him back, as if she had to have Samuel beside her at all times.

I heard murmurs ripple through the crowd. I could imagine what they were whispering. I'm sure they were wondering where she'd come from, why Samuel had chosen to escort her to the benefit. If only they'd known her less than a week ago, before she'd been forced to drink Oliver's blood. If only they knew the man on her arm was evil incarnate. And if only they knew that vampires walked among them—and that some were capable of far more destruction than they could even imagine.

"Violet!" I heard a shriek as I saw Cora spring from her chair at the far end of the room and run toward her sister. Luckily, the band had resumed and the ballroom was abuzz with chattering, glass clinking, and footsteps. No one had heard her outburst except a few girls sitting nearby. But even that was too many. Any attention drawn to Cora, or to us, put our plan at risk.

"No!" Damon and I yelled at the same time, racing into the crush of bodies that separated us from Cora. But Damon was faster, and instantly, he was by her side. He seized her arm with one hand and covered her mouth with the other. "Be quiet!" he ordered, wrestling her back into her chair. Then, he leaned in front of her, his hands clasped in prayer.

"She's hysterical," he said, loudly enough so the girls and Sister Benedict could hear. "It sometimes happens when young women aren't accustomed to large crowds. We'll say an extra prayer for her," Damon added as I joined him in front of Cora.

"What were you trying to do?" I hissed. She winced at my harsh tone. I glanced over my shoulder to see if Violet had heard Cora's cry. Luckily, she was at the opposite end of the room, curtseying in front of a tall, thin man whom I vaguely recognized as the Lord Mayor of London.

"I'm sorry!" Cora whispered, the color draining from her face. She pulled a handkerchief from her pocket and twisted it in her hands, staring intently at the fabric instead of me. "I don't know what came over me. I just saw Violet and was so happy to see her . . . I'm sorry."

"It's fine," I said. I shot Damon a look. The plan was still in place. Everything would be *fine*.

"He's right," Damon said. "You weren't even that loud. I've heard Stefan scream louder at his own shadow," Damon quipped.

A glimmer of a smile crossed Cora's face. I suppose she felt that if Damon and I were still engaging in civil banter, everything would be all right. She puffed out her cheeks and exhaled. "Do you think she knows I'm here?" she asked, her eyes searching mine.

"Vampires have good senses, but they aren't telepathic. They can't tell where someone else is unless they hear or see them," I explained. "Now, please remember that the quieter you are, the better chance we have of getting Violet." I locked eyes with her and nodded, reassuring her that we could still do this. Her determined expression reminded me so much of Oliver's when he would try to convince me to take him hunting that my heart clenched.

I looked back at the crowd. Violet was still deep in conversation with the Lord Mayor, but Samuel had left her side. I saw that he was now clasping hands with Sister Benedict, only a few paces away from me. I froze, panic setting in as I imagined him asking about the pair of monks who weren't on the approved invitee list.

But then, Sister Benedict ushered him into the crowd of Asylum girls. He tapped one on the shoulder. She was stocky, with brown hair that grazed her shoulders and large, doelike brown eyes.

I sucked in my breath as I placed a warning hand on Damon's shoulder. I didn't trust him not to try to surprise Samuel. But he stayed by my side silently. One by one, Samuel picked his victims and escorted them toward the back of the ballroom.

"It's time," I whispered to Cora.

She nodded, her large eyes shining. "Good luck."

I smiled confidently. I didn't need luck anymore. I had a foolproof plan and revenge-hungry Damon on my side. Now all we needed to do was fight for our freedom.

12

amon and I hurried after Samuel, following him into the cavernous servant area across from the ballroom. Moss grew from crevices in the walls, and the hallway smelled damp—almost like a swamp. Samuel had ducked out of sight into one of the wooden doors dotting either side of the hall. I had no idea where he could be. I tested one of doorknobs. Locked.

I zigzagged farther down the corridor, putting my weight against each door until I heard a blood-curdling, otherworldly scream coming from the far end of the hall. It echoed in my bones and made me certain the plan had worked. Anticipation buzzed in my veins.

"Ready, brother?" Damon whispered. His eyes were red with anger. We ran, side by side, following the sound of the cry.

Damon used his brute strength to bust through the locked door. Inside, Samuel lay on the ground, writhing and clutching his gut as if his insides were on fire. Surrounding him were four terrified and bewildered Asylum girls. One girl was clutching her neck as blood seeped through her fingers, while the other three were gathered around her. The four whitewashed walls were empty except for a single wooden cross, and a lone candle burned on a wooden table, casting an eerie glow on the scene. We were far enough away from the party that no one could hear us, which I suppose was why Samuel had chosen this room in the first place. He'd probably brought girls here during every Magdalene Asylum fundraising ball.

"Run!" I barked to the girls. They didn't need any more urging. One by one, they took off down the corridor. I wondered what they would say to Sister Agatha, but brushed the thought away. We were on borrowed time, and I knew it was imperative we kill Samuel right away.

He was completely at our mercy, and we were ready to strike.

"Not so powerful now, are you?" Damon sneered, reaching into the folds of his cloak for a wooden cross he must have been planning to use as a stake. He let loose a low, demonic laugh and I stepped back. I may have been after Samuel's life, but Damon seemed to be after something more. He wasn't just intending to kill Samuel. He was intending to torture him.

"You think you can destroy me with that?" Samuel gasped, mustering a weak laugh.

Just as Damon reared back, ready to strike, Samuel lunged to his feet, pushing him against the wall. The cross clattered to the floor. I grabbed it, slashing at the air. But Samuel's quick movement had extinguished the candle lighting the room, and as we were plunged into darkness, Samuel struck. I felt a searing pain below my knee and staggered onto my back, suddenly unable to move. A stake was jutting out from under my kneecap.

I couldn't muster the strength to pull myself into a seated position to yank it out. I twisted, trying to get a view of the room. Samuel and Damon were circling each other. Damon's jaw was clenched and blood was running down his face.

Kill him, I willed. *No torture. Just strike. You don't have time.*

In my pain, I couldn't be sure whether I was saying the words or merely thinking them. But I heard Damon's low, mocking laugh.

"Ready to be revealed as a monster? What will Lord Ainsley think? Better call in all your political favors now," Damon said. "Unless I just kill you. Take you off their hands."

Just kill him, I thought desperately.

Samuel turned toward me—that time, I'd spoken aloud. "I'm afraid your brother won't be killing me," he said evenly as he pulled a glittering, jewel-encrusted knife from his jacket. The sound of sizzling flesh assaulted my ears; I could tell the knife had been dipped in vervain.

"Damon!" I yelled, but it was too late. Samuel took the knife and shoved it into Damon's abdomen. Blood immediately seeped through his robes.

Samuel looked back and forth at us both, his eyes glittering in the darkness. I glared at him, still unable to move. He continued to laugh, a low, dangerous sound, as ominous as an earthquake.

"I have to hand it to you, boys," he said, tapping his long fingers together and pacing the room. I wondered if this was when he'd strike, or if he'd hold out. "You tried valiantly. I didn't think you had it in you. Spiking those little brats with vervain was admirable. But unfortunately, I have quite a bit of vervain in me. Started dosing myself with it years ago. Nasty and unpleasant, yes, but it does help build immunity." He wiped his mouth with his handkerchief. "See, not so much the worse for wear." He clapped his hands together, causing dried red flecks of blood to fall to the ground like rain.

"Which is more than I can say for your little friends," he continued. "You think you're the only ones who can spoil an evening? Jack the Ripper knows how it's done.

Now seems like the perfect time for him to head back to Whitechapel and strike again. The only question is, in a benefit full of whores, who will be the lucky lady?" Samuel's mouth twisted into a sickening grin.

"No," I said, as the horror of it invaded my imagination. I pictured one of the Asylum girls, ripped from the inside out. My leg was hurting badly, and I knew I'd lost a lot of blood. But my injuries were nothing compared to what Samuel would do to those girls. Cora was out there, alone . . .

I lurched upright, pulling at the stake in my shin.

Samuel laughed at my lame attempt at stopping him. "It's been a pleasure, boys," he said as he turned to leave.

I glanced over at Damon, crumpled on the floor. Blood was trickling out of his stomach. I yanked again, but the stake in my leg wouldn't budge. Instead, every attempt to pull it out caused me to fall back in spasms of agony.

Far in the distance, I heard the faint strains of a waltz in the ballroom, and the cheerful chatter of the partygoers, completely unaware of the demon in their midst.

13

few agonizing minutes later, I managed to yank the stake from my knee and stanched the wound with a stretch of fabric ripped from my robe. I stood up and hobbled across the dark room toward Damon. My leg seemed all right, considering the bone had been broken only minutes before. My body healed fast and already I could tell my knee was on the mend. But Damon . . . he was still on the ground in agony, blood gushing from his gut even as he tried to stand. This wasn't an injury he'd be able to walk off. I debated: Should I leave him here and run to Whitechapel? Or was Samuel's challenge a trap? I couldn't think clearly, but I could sense the moments counting down. A girl's blood would be on my hands if I didn't act fast—and make the right decision—soon.

Cora burst into the room. Her face paled as she took in the sight of us, but she moved forward purposefully.

"What happened?" she asked as she sank to the floor beside Damon. "Is he . . ."

"Samuel stabbed him. Vervain. He'll be all right eventually."

"What can I do?" she asked, looking down at him.

I hesitated. I knew Damon was in bad shape, but without him I would not be able to stop Samuel from killing again tonight. And I knew what Damon needed. I would not force her, but if she did it willingly . . . "You could give him your blood," I said.

Cora's hands flew to her throat. "But where . . . how?" Cora asked.

"I just need your wrist. Not a lot. Do you trust me?"

Cora nodded silently, took off her vervain charm, and held out her white wrist. Even after living in the Asylum, Cora's skin smelled like an intoxicating combination of freesia and milk.

I took a step back. I didn't want to be tempted. Instead, I took the blood-covered knife, wiped it on the sleeve of my robe to remove any vervain left on its surface, and handed it to her.

"Just a small cut will do. Not too much—he has to be able to stop," I cautioned.

Without hesitation, Cora took the knife and held it

against her skin, pushing until she created a long, clean channel of blood.

"Good," I said. "Now let him drink."

At first, Damon tentatively licked Cora's wrist, but then began sucking harder and more insistently. I turned away, part of me jealous that Damon was able to experience Cora's sweetness in a way that I would never allow myself to.

"That's enough!" I said desperately. There was such a fine line between life and death.

Damon glanced up at me and raised his eyebrows.

"Did you see him?" he asked Cora after briefly kissing her wrist in thanks.

"Yes." Cora nodded, eyes wide. "And he took Elizabeth and Cathy! Just walked out the door with them, and no one said a word. I came down here as fast as I could. I knew I couldn't go after him alone." Cora's voice was unnaturally high.

"He's got them," Damon said darkly, as if it were a point of fact. He was standing now and looked as strong as ever, except for the large red bloodstain on his robe.

Cora sniffed. "Elizabeth and Cathy drank the vervain. So they'll be all right, won't they?" she asked in a small voice.

"Vervain doesn't work on Samuel," I said. "He's been dosing *himself*. We need to follow them." I didn't tell her about Samuel's demonic wager. I couldn't.

"We need to find them." Damon's mouth was set. "Another Jack the Ripper attack will happen tonight. He knows we're here. And he won't stop killing until the trail of blood leads the police to us."

Damon took a distraught Cora under his arm and led her out of the room.

We left through a back entrance, and the three of us ran through the streets for what felt like an eternity. The wind was howling, and the party seemed ages away. As we pelted toward the rain-soaked alleys of Whitechapel, I felt as if we'd been transported back to Mystic Falls after the vampire siege, when the entire town had smelled of vervain, fire, blood, and death. Except Whitechapel was filled with snaking side streets and tiny courtyards masked by towering boardinghouses. It would be impossible to find Samuel in time. And yet, we *had* to.

I sniffed the air to pick out Samuel's direction. The wind carried the unmistakable scent of blood toward us. It was so strong my fangs automatically bulged under my gums.

We were too late.

Rushing toward source of the smell, I saw movement at the center of the square.

"He's here," Damon said tersely.

I nodded, freezing in my tracks.

Then another sound captured my attention. I might

have chalked it up to the wind, whistling through the narrow alleys, but Damon had heard it, too. He sprang toward the end of the alley. I urged Cora to stay put before following him.

And there, I saw him. Lit by a thin sliver of moonlight was Henry. A knife glittered in his hand, dripping with blood. Below him lay the prone body of Cathy, the Asylum girl who'd befriended Cora.

My stomach lurched. I'd been responsible for dozens of deaths, and I'd seen terrible vampire murders. But I'd never seen a death like this. It brought me back two decades to the Sutherlands' well-maintained living room. There, the entrails of every member of the Sutherland family were spattered across the walls and the floor, making it impossible to tell which body part originally belonged to whom.

And here, Cathy's guts were being splayed out onto the street. Henry seemed entranced by the gore. Most vampires killed cleanly, draining blood from two small holes in the neck. But Henry had split open Cathy's entire body, and had made slash after slash across her neck. Her clothing was so bloodstained that it was impossible to ascertain the original color of her dress. This was the work of a deranged demon.

Henry looked up. I was sure he knew what a picture he was painting for us, bowed over his prey. "Why, hello.

I'm afraid you're late for dinner. I would have whipped up a dessert, but my brother told me this blood was ruined for vampire consumption. What a waste." Henry leered at us. Then he stood and lunged toward Damon.

Damon sidestepped him, causing Henry to ricochet against the wall. He fell to the ground, but quickly bounced back up, laughing demonically. With Damon occupying his attention, I rushed to check on Cathy to see if anything could be done.

I knelt beside her body, thankful that she was dead, not alive and in agony. Hopefully the death had been quick. Then I thought about Elizabeth, too, who might not have been so lucky. Chances were, since she wasn't here now, she'd already met her fate.

"Good luck trying to fix that mess," a smooth, low voice said behind me. "I'd say better luck next time, but there won't be one."

I whirled around. It was Samuel, a snow-white handkerchief tucked in his jacket pocket and a half smile on his face.

"I'm surprised you're so disgusted. I do know how fond you and your brother are of messes. Isn't that what you both have been doing since you arrived in London? Finding yourselves in impossible situations? It's as if you two have a death wish." Samuel shook his head. "In a way, it's too easy," he mused, kneeling down and smoothing

Cathy's hair back from her pale face as tenderly as a husband caressing his bride. From the neck up, she looked as if she was merely sleeping.

I leaped toward Samuel, guided by instinct as I threw a wild punch. My fist hit flesh, and Samuel staggered back. Maybe the vervain had affected him more than I thought. I wound up, ready to hit again, when a wild, raw scream rang out behind me. I whirled around and saw Cora next to Cathy's body. Seeing her face, tortured by the sight of her friend ripped to pieces, I hurried to her side, my fight with Samuel all but forgotten.

Samuel, standing tall and strong as ever, turned toward Cora, a bemused expression on his face. "So, shall I kill your little friend? Or make her one of us?" Samuel asked as he pulled out a gold pocket watch and noted the time, smiling in satisfaction. I pulled Cora closer to me. "By my account, the Whitechapel Vigilance Committee should be here in minutes. I've been asking them to patrol Mitre Square every hour, on the hour. I always thought it was the perfect place for a careless killer to be caught. So you'll forgive me if I break up the games," he said. He whistled once. Henry looked up from his scuffle with Damon and immediately raced to his brother's side. "They'll appreciate catching the killers red-handed. Take it like men, will you?" With that, Samuel grabbed the back of Damon's neck and forced his face into Cathy's innards. Cora moaned in dismay, and I felt my own insides twist.

Damon choked as the vervain in Cathy's body hit his lips and tried to jerk back, sputtering in equal parts anger and agony.

"Stefan? A snack?" Samuel asked, cackling, then shook his head as if he'd thought better of it. "No, too easy. And too unkind. I know how your brother abhors sharing the spotlight. Just like he abhors sharing his women. Katherine would always relay how humorous it was to pit the two of you against each other and watch you fight for her affections. As if either of you ever *could* have won her hand," he laughed, as a peal of police bells pierced the night air and candlelight appeared in the windows of the buildings facing the square. Curious faces peeked out, and I knew we had only seconds to escape.

"I'll see you soon, Stefan. And Damon, enjoy your demise," Samuel said, releasing Damon's neck. He seized Henry by the arm and they took off around the corner. The Whitechapel Vigilance Committee was coming, and Damon was again weakened by vervain. Still, I yanked him to his feet and searched for an escape route. A narrow path ran between two houses nearby. That would have to do.

"We can't just *leave* her!" Cora shouted, staring at Cathy's mutilated body in despair.

"Cora, we have to go!" I said, grabbing her shoulders and shaking her slightly. I didn't want to hurt her, but I needed her to pay attention. If Cora became hysterical, none of us would be safe.

Cora straightened her shoulders and pressed her lips together in a tight line. A single tear trickled from the corner of her eye. She didn't bother wiping it away.

"I'm fine," she said, nodding her head as if willing it to be true. I dragged Damon with me alongside Cora as we ran, winding down one alley and another until we came to a tiny passageway between streets, filled with refuse and rats.

"Here," Cora said, walking midway down the street and throwing her shoulder against a wooden door. Nothing. I stepped in front of her and tried again. It swung open easily.

As soon as we walked inside, I heard rats scurrying and bats squeaking. The structure seemed to have been a milliner's shop at some point, and dusty hats and dresses hung from racks, rotting. I quickly located a heavy black trunk and dragged it in front of the door.

"We're safe," Cora said flatly, sinking to the ground and hugging her knees to her chest.

I was about to breathe a sigh of relief when I felt myself pinned to the wall by an unseen hand. I looked around wildly and realized the hand was connected to Damon. He squeezed my neck and scowled at me, hatred evident in his dark eyes.

"What now?" I asked, pushing him away. We had two vampires on our trail, a vigilance committee after us, and a cadre of policemen looking for us. Damon had the blood of an innocent girl all over his face. Yet all he seemed to be concerned with was reigniting our years-old feud.

"Well, Stefan," Damon said, practically spitting out the words. "How do you feel about your grand plans now? Two more of your precious humans are dead, and not only are the police after me, but a Vigilance Committee is likely coming for me with torches and handcuffs. And instead of trying to destroy Henry or Samuel, trying to help me in the fight, all you cared about was how Cora *felt*." Damon released his grip but kept his eyes locked on me. "You have no idea how to be a vampire. You have no idea how to fight. And I'm tired of listening to you."

"I'm sorry," Cora said in a small voice. "I should have been braver."

"You should have been nothing," Damon spat. "You shouldn't even have been there. This is our world, and Stefan can't seem to understand that he needs to live in it. All he wants to do is orchestrate events to his liking. He's been telling me what to do since we got to London, and like an idiot, I've listened to him. But I'm not listening anymore," Damon said. "We're done."

The words were like a knife to my stomach.

"Do you think I like living in tunnels and feeling like I'm hunted? Do you think I *like* seeing innocent humans die? I'm doing this to help you," I shouted.

"How many times do I have to tell you? I don't want your help," Damon hissed, his voice low and ominous. "I didn't need your help when we were humans, and I don't need your help now. We're done, brother. We're done forever."

"Fine!" I yelled. It was petulant and pathetic, but it was true. Because we *were* done. I didn't want to worry and plan and always, endlessly, feel unappreciated and useless. I may have put up with that when I was a human, forever the younger brother trailing, puppylike, behind Damon. But not anymore. "Go."

With that, Damon stormed out of the decrepit shop, batting the trunk away from the door as if it weighed nothing. I slammed the door behind him. If he wanted to run right into the arms of the Whitechapel Vigilance Committee, then let him go ahead. We were done. My thoughts were interrupted by a whimper from Cora. I placed a hand on her arm, knowing it wouldn't do much to comfort her.

"It's all right," I said, even though it wasn't. I felt the beginnings of a headache throbbing at my temples. Damon was gone, and it sounded like he was gone for good. And I didn't blame him. I'd been angry with him in the past, but this was the first time I'd told him to go.

Good riddance, I thought, willing myself to believe it, trying to cast Damon as just another ill-mannered vampire, like the ones I'd lived with in New Orleans.

But he wasn't. It was the same damning conclusion I'd always reached: Blood mattered. Damon mattered. Even if I wished he didn't.

The sound of police bells drew closer, and I could hear footsteps. Torchlight danced along the whitewashed walls of the millinery shop, and once again I was thankful for Cora's quick thinking.

Just then, we heard a cry from outside, so loud it rattled the windows, followed by the sound of doors slamming and footsteps echoing on the pavement.

"They found Cathy," Cora noted, her voice devoid of emotion. I nodded helplessly. "I wonder where Elizabeth is. She can't be alive, can she?"

"No." I shook my head. Saying anything else would imply that I had hope. And I didn't. The world was evil—I was evil—and everything I touched became surrounded by blood, destruction, and chaos. Including Cora. It was no way to live.

"It's hard, isn't it," Cora said softly in the darkness.

"What is?" I asked.

"Living," she replied. "It's harder than death, I think.

Because the first thing I thought when I saw Cathy was how lucky she was. She doesn't have to live through this. She doesn't have to see her friends torn apart, and she doesn't have to live with any regret for bringing them into her problems. She's free. It's a wicked thought, isn't it?" Cora asked.

"No, it's the truth. I think it's what Damon believes, too," I admitted. I remembered when he had begged for the death I refused to give to him. Was that the root of all our problems? And if so, what could I do for forgiveness? In the moment when Cora's terrified shriek pierced the night air, I had gone to her without a second thought. But in doing so, I had betrayed Damon, scuffling with Henry nearby. Damon on his own in London was as good as dead. If Samuel didn't get him, then the Whitechapel Vigilance Committee would.

"You know he wasn't mad at you tonight. That was just an excuse."

"Maybe he was right. You chose me," Cora said in a small voice.

"I didn't choose anyone. Damon can look out for himself. You . . ."

"Can't?" Cora asked, with a raw laugh.

" . . . just saw your friend dead on the street," I finished. "But no. Damon's always looking for a reason to hate me. And . . ." I took a deep breath. "Maybe he should. Because you see, I loved my brother. And when I became a vampire, I wanted him with me. I forced him to turn against his will. He was fighting his transition and I made him drink human blood. And he'll never, ever forgive me for that."

"I don't think that I would hate Violet if she turned me," Cora mused. "I think if I knew she did it for the right reasons, I would understand and forgive her. At least we'd be together."

"It's not that simple," I said after a moment.

We were quiet for some time. Through the grime coating the shop windows, I could see the faintest streaks of sunlight appearing like brushstrokes against the inky black sky. The worst of the night was behind us.

"Nothing that's worth it is ever simple," Cora said in the darkness, picking up our earlier conversation and yanking me back to the present.

"Hmm?" I asked, startled.

"Nothing that's worth anything is ever simple. That's what makes it worth it. That's what Violet always used to say when things got hard for us. She was the one who pushed for us to move to London. I'd have been happy to stay in Donegal, settle down . . ." Cora sighed. "Violet convinced our parents to let us move. And right before we boarded the boat, my da took me by the shoulders and told me to look after his little girl."

"You did the best you could."

Cora shook her head. "I didn't! I was charmed by Samuel the second he came into the Ten Bells. He sat at the bar and told me I was beautiful. I didn't give a second thought to what would happen to Violet when I went with him. And then . . . I was so stupid!" she exploded angrily. "Why couldn't I resist him? I knew well enough that no nobleman like him would want a girl like me, so why couldn't I ignore the compulsion?"

I pulled her toward me, rocking her back and forth in my arms. "There is no way you could have fought the compulsion without vervain. It wasn't your fault," I said soothingly. She relaxed against my chest. I noticed a crease between her eyes that hadn't been there a few days earlier. She looked exhausted, and I wanted to do everything in my power to make her pain and hurt and confusion go away. But I couldn't.

"So many men are out there looking for girls just like you. You're amazing," I said, brushing the hair back from her eyes. I didn't love her, at least not in the way that causes a human heart to flutter with anticipation. But what I felt for her was deep and sincere: It was as if we were soul mates in the strictest sense of the word, bound by duty to our kin and willing to do anything in the face of evil. She was a true friend. And I hoped she could tell how much I valued her.

"Thanks," she said wryly, tilting her chin up to me.

Her angular face was bathed in a swath of early morning light coming through a crack in the window. "How can I go wrong when I have the approval of vampires?"

I chuckled. It wasn't funny, not really, but as I continued to laugh, a giggle rose from Cora's lips.

"Shh!" I exclaimed, pressing my hand to her mouth.

"I can't!" she said, still laughing. Tears sprang from her eyes and leaked down her cheeks, and I knew it wasn't the joke making her cry. I held her tighter and let her tears wash over me. The world was a harsh place to live in, but here and now, at least we had each other.

14

I fell asleep listening to the *ba-dum, ba-dum* of Cora's heartbeat. It was rhythmic and steady, a metronomic reminder that not all was lost. And somehow, the sound got me through the night.

I awoke to thin rays of light seeping through the grime-caked windows. I blanched as I blinked at my surroundings. The wooden floor was covered with dust, and I could see the paw prints and tail marks of rats. Cockroaches scurried along the baseboards.

"Wake up," I whispered, nudging Cora's shoulder. Her hands were clasped together as though in prayer.

Cora blinked up at me. The shadows under her eyes were so dark and pronounced it was as if she'd drawn them with kohl. Her smock had shifted as she slept, exposing her frail collarbone. I hated to wake her, bring her back into this horrible reality.

"Good morning," I whispered. "How did you sleep?"

"Better than I imagined, considering the circumstances," Cora said in a small voice, sitting up.

"I know," I said. "But the good news is we're here, and we're safe. And everything's always better in the morning." I smiled despite myself. It was a phrase my mother had used when I was a child, worried about monsters hiding under my bed. Only now, the monsters weren't hiding.

"What are we going to do?" she asked.

"We'll think of something. It will be fine," I said. That had been my go-to phrase for the past few days, and I was sure Cora was just as tired of hearing it as I was of saying it. Every plan I thought of was more fantastical and useless than the last. My mind felt overworked and unwieldy. But what could we do? Vervain wouldn't hurt Samuel, and he had the entire London police force wrapped around his little finger.

My mind drifted to Katherine. Samuel had been right; she'd delighted in pitting Damon and me against each other. I wanted to get into Katherine's brain and try to imagine what she would do in my circumstances. Maybe that was the answer. What better way to fight a maniacal vampire than to think like one myself?

Katherine, though, was hardly alone. And not just with

her abundance of male suitors. She had her maidservant, Emily, by her side. Emily, who was also a witch. She'd perform spells for Katherine, giving her an advantage over humans and vampires both.

I needed something beyond the Power I had as a vampire. I needed to talk to James.

"What's that?" Cora asked nervously, pulling me out of my reverie. Something was scuttling around behind a moldering hatbox in the corner and Cora was looking around the shop as though expecting to find one of the mannequins had come to life. Remarkably, the abandoned store was more frightening in the weak light of day than it had been in darkness.

"Let's go. I have an idea," I said.

She stood up and brushed off her dress. She looked exhausted and dirty, but resolute. Despite everything she had seen, she was choosing to move forward and keep fighting. And that inspired me. If Cora was strong enough to stare down impossible odds, I was going to make sure she survived to have a long and fulfilling life.

When we reached the Emporium, I rapped three times, listening for sounds on the other side of the door.

"Who's there?" James called. I heard jars rattling about.

"It's Stefan, Damon's brother," I replied. Sometimes, my relationship to Damon came in handy, I had to admit.

Finally, James opened the door. His good eye was oozing even more than it had been the other day, and he looked right past me to Cora.

"What's she doing here?" he asked suspiciously.

"She's all right. She's a friend," I answered.

"A human? I swear, some vampires never learn," he said roughly, but he hustled us inside the tiny shop. He locked eyes with me. "You need goat's blood tea. On the house. I like to do my best customers favors, because I know it'll come back to me in some way. And you certainly helped me get rid of my back inventory of vervain." He gestured to a small table in the corner, waving us to sit down.

I shifted uncomfortably from one foot to the other, unsure of how to tell him what had actually happened with the vervain. I decided to stall, hoping that the magic-infused products lining the shelves would inspire a new plan. "Tea would be terrific."

James bustled around in the back of the shop as Cora and I sat at the rickety table.

"A special drink for the miss," James said as he returned, offering Cora a steaming mug of broth. "It has rhinoceros horn flakes. Good for bravery," he explained solemnly. Cora clutched the cup with two hands and took a tiny sip.

"It's good," Cora said. "It just tastes like the Irish tea back home."

"Well, you're not here for tea, so let's talk," James said,

taking a seat behind the counter and draining his own mug. "Where's your brother?"

I chose my words carefully. "He's on a different path now," I said. That much was true. Whether the road was leading to destruction, I was trying not to think. "But we need your help. The Jack the Ripper murders are being committed by a demented vampire. London is in danger."

"London's in danger?" James asked skeptically, crossing his arms over his chest. "London's always in danger. For the past thousand years, people have been saying that, and yet the city is still standing. And why should I care about the current crisis? There'll just be another one after it."

I racked my brain. It was true. Why *should* he care? He was unconcerned with petty fights between vampires. If anything, he'd *prefer* a feud—more income for him.

"Because you're a good man," Cora said simply. "Just like Stefan. Please help us."

James laughed. He slid off his stool and circled Cora.

"I'm a good man? No, sweetheart, I'm an awful man who's seen and done some terrible things. But I like your innocence. You probably think there's hope for the world yet."

"There *is* hope," Cora said, her voice strong and steady.

James nodded. "I think you have a touch of witch in you. It's very slight, must've been an ancestor way back, but it's somewhere in there."

"Do you have anything else that hurts vampires?" I interjected. "The vervain didn't work. Samuel . . . the vampire . . . has been dosing himself to build up immunity."

"Smart bloke," James said to himself. "Most of you vampires are too bloodthirsty, too focused on your next meal to see the bigger picture. But maybe some of you are beginning to think things through. Dosing with vervain, I hadn't thought of that. And I certainly never imagined seeing a vampire like you with a human girl on his arm. And you haven't even been feeding on her or compelling her. Remarkable," James said, shaking his head.

"So can you help us?" Cora asked.

"Well, I'm afraid I've nothing here that would block a determined vampire," he said, glancing up at a dusty bookshelf and running his finger along the titles.

"Oh," I said, my heart falling. "Well, then, thank you very much for your—"

"Hang on!" James said indignantly. "*Listen*. That's the trouble with you vampires. Always jumping to conclusions without hearing the whole story. That's why I prefer witches myself. They *think*. Now, I said *I* didn't have anything. But I didn't say it didn't exist."

"What do you mean?" I asked slowly.

"Now, normally I wouldn't consider him for you—he hates vampires with a passion and hasn't been the same since one threw him off London Bridge—but since you're desperate . . . he *is* good in a crisis . . ." James trailed off, thinking.

"Who is?" I asked urgently.

"Ephraim," James whispered, as though it were an incantation.

"Who?" It was as if he'd mentioned God or Lucifer or another entity I should have been on a first-name basis with.

"Ephraim. He's a dangerous, powerful witch. Or was in his time. But then he got too greedy. Demons from all over the world sought him out, and he'd perform his spells for whoever had the money, no matter whether the person was on the side of good or evil. Of course, he charged the witches a little less and the vampires a little more, but he'd do work for anyone. Lately, though . . . people say he's changed. But his power hasn't ebbed. If anything, he's stronger than ever."

"Ephraim," Cora repeated. "Where is he?"

"Top of Big Ben," James answered. "But you have to time it right. I suppose it's why people call it the witching hour. When the clock strikes twelve, you can find him. He'll be expecting you."

"Midnight at Big Ben. We'll be there," I agreed quickly.

"Good. Because he doesn't like waiting. Makes him nervous. Now, make sure no one sees or follows you. At the far end of the tower, there's a tunnel. It's unguarded at all times," James said, nodding as he pulled a rumpled piece of paper from a drawer and handed it to Cora. "The instructions should be clear enough. Give this paper to him so he'll know I sent you. Consider it your admission ticket."

Cora shoved the paper into her coat pocket.

"I warn you, Ephraim will ask for payment. Not necessarily cash. But there's always a price to pay."

"I understand," I said. "Thank you."

"Don't thank me yet," James warned. "I've been around a lot longer than you. Remember, even if you have an antidote, it doesn't mean the poison won't kill you." He stared glumly into his tea. "There's been a war between good and evil raging on for years. Sometimes good wins, sometimes evil wins. It's a coin toss." As if to prove his point, he pulled a hexagonal coin from his pocket— I instantly recognized it as the one that had bought me a meal of Bengal tiger blood. He threw the coin into the air and the three of us watched it fall to the table. It landed on a side that had a complicated geometric pattern. I pulled the coin toward me and flipped it over. The other side showed the same pattern.

"Which side is which?" I asked in confusion.

James smiled. "Sometimes no one knows," he said.

Of course. I tried to contain my frustration, but it was hard. I hadn't come here for riddles—I came for answers. But all I was leaving with were more questions. More questions, a double-faced coin, a scrap of paper, and a mysterious name.

"Come on," Cora said, sliding her chair away from the table and placing a hand on my shoulder. "And thank you," she said to James.

We exited the shop. In the street, I turned back to look at it. The window was frosted and filled with cobwebs, the door covered over with boards; anyone walking by would think the building was abandoned. But wasn't that just another one of James's lessons? It was one I understood: Nothing is what it seems. But in this case, we were clearly on the side of good. I only hoped Ephraim would be more sympathetic to our position than James was. Because right now, this vampire-loathing witch was our only hope.

15

Cora and I avoided the tunnel for the rest of the afternoon. Without Damon, it felt too silent and empty. Instead, we wandered the streets of London as Cora told me stories about its history: that a fire had ravaged the entire city hundreds of years ago, that ravens were kept in the Tower of London in a superstitious effort to ward against the city's destruction, and that human bodies had been sacrificed to London Bridge so it would never collapse. I wasn't sure whether the stories were true or pulled from her imagination, but I liked listening to her lilting Irish accent. They distracted us, and I knew we both needed distraction from the very real horrors we'd encountered in this city.

But finally, we'd reached our destination: Big Ben. We arrived just as the magnificent tower clock read eleven-thirty. The structure was imposing; all sharp angles and hard surfaces. Nearby was the river, and Parliament, while Westminster Abbey was a stone's throw away. I knew now why Big Ben was an iconic symbol of London.

"And here concludes our tour," Cora said, gazing up at it in reverence. "I've never been here before."

Surrounding the building were soldiers wearing red uniforms and black hats. Even at this late hour, they were standing sharply at attention, their eyes trained on the silent street. A lone boat sailed down the river. It looked empty, and I remembered one of the stories Cora had told me as we were walking along the docks, about ghost ships in the time of pirates on the high seas. I shivered.

Cora pulled out the worn piece of paper James had given her and smoothed it against her knee before reading aloud:

"Although it may be called Big Ben
And ring'd around by guardsmen
Take note of the things that aren't meant to be seen
Unlike an entrance fit for a Queen
Think like a mouse or rat or flea
And at Ephraim's entrance you'll be."

"Where do you think it is?" Cora asked.

"Somewhere low to the ground, most likely," I said.

I loved poetry, but it had been a while since my last encounter with nursery rhymes. We circled the clock twice, scanning the ground for an entrance. I'd had no idea Big Ben would be so heavily guarded. I'd become used to London being deserted at night. But there seemed to be no way to bypass the guards.

"*Things that aren't meant to be seen* . . ." Cora trailed off, lost in thought. "Do you think that would be the back of the clock? That's something that's always hidden, right?"

Just then, the clock struck twelve.

"We don't have much time," Cora said. As the guards marched in formation for the traditional changing of the guard, we headed to the back of the hulking stone edifice. The clock tower was connected to the sprawling structure of the Palace of Westminster, and up close I could make out numerous cracks in the limestone.

"Look!" Cora called in excitement. She clapped a hand over her mouth. "Sorry," she said abashedly. "It's just . . . there's a hole there," she said, pointing to a crack at the base of the tower.

"Cora, I'm a vampire, not an elf." The entrance, if that was what it was, couldn't have been more than a foot high. It was a triangular gap where one limestone block had become loose from its neighbor.

Cora gave me a quick smile before crouching down and sticking her hand inside the hole. "I'm going to try it," she said. So subtly I assumed it was a trick of the light, the hole began to grow. Cora put her arm farther in, and the hole grew bigger still. She turned to me, eyebrow raised.

Ephraim *must* be powerful to have such an enchanted entrance to his lair.

"I'll go first," I decided. I slid inside and Cora followed. We found ourselves in a narrow tunnel facing a winding set of stairs that seemed to rise to the heavens. Silently, we began to ascend.

"Stefan," Cora said, her voice wavering. "What if this is a mistake? What if Ephraim is beyond reason?"

"It'll be all right. We're almost there," I said, even though I had no idea. I wondered if the stairs, too, were not what they seemed. For all I knew, they were rotating below our feet, keeping us suspended in darkness while we climbed endlessly. Anything was possible.

Just as I was considering the worst, the stairs ended abruptly. We faced an iron door. I pushed at it tentatively, not sure if we were going to set off a trap or burst into flames.

"Who goes there?" a voice boomed, seeming to come from all places at once.

"I come as a friend," I said, suddenly calm. We were here now and there was no backing out, so what would be would be.

I glanced at our surroundings. The room was tiny and

octagonal. At most, it could hold five people, and I had to duck to keep my head from grazing the sloping, cob-webbed stone ceiling. The voice had come from a man sitting on a lone concrete block in the center of the tiny room. Burning candles dotted the damp floor, and a single opening, no larger than a brick, was cut into one wall. Through it, all of London was laid out beneath us. Across from us was another archway, which must have held the clock itself. I could see the large brass elements moving ponderously around an enormous circle. I wondered why Ephraim had chosen to reside in Big Ben, and if anyone knew he lived here.

The man turned from the window. He looked to be in his fifties and wore a tattered robe. Unlike James, he wouldn't stand out as grotesque on the streets, although there was something about his bearing that would unnerve strangers—a nervous tension resonating throughout his body, giving the sense that he was always on high alert, prepared to attack or flee at a moment's notice.

He eased toward me, sniffing the air as though he were a dog meeting another dog on the road. With James's warnings in mind, I stood still, allowing him to continue this unorthodox mode of introduction. Cora remained at my side, her hands clasped demurely at her waist.

"She's a human?" the man asked. "Ephraim likes humans. Ephraim *doesn't* like vampires."

Cora stepped forward. "Yes," she said with a slight nod, causing her hair to fall over her eyes. "I am a human, but Stefan is not a typical vampire."

"Ephraim will be the judge of that."

"Can we speak with Ephraim?"

I heard a cawing sound as a large black raven flapped its wings and flew from a corner onto the man's shoulder. I remembered the story Cora had told me: If the ravens were ever to leave the Tower of London, then all of England would fall. I wondered if the same were true of Ephraim in Big Ben. Maybe he was embedded there, stuck forever in the lore and legend of England. I felt the hairs rise on the back of my neck.

The man regarded the raven thoughtfully, then turned back to us.

"I am Ephraim," he proclaimed. "Why have you come?"

"Vampires," I said simply.

"Vampires!" Ephraim spat. He gently stroked the raven's wing with two of his swollen, misshapen fingers. While his face appeared middle-aged, his hands looked as withered and gnarled as the branches of an ancient oak. "Vampires remind Ephraim of leeches. And Ephraim knows leeches are good for spells, but not for company."

While James had not underestimated Ephraim's animosity toward vampires, I wondered if he had perhaps underestimated his madness.

"You don't know him," Cora said; her voice was clear as a clarion.

Ephraim chuckled. "We don't know him!" he said to the raven in a singsong voice.

"Good morning!" the raven croaked, in such a perfect English accent that I blinked in surprise.

"He's a good man," Cora continued, unperturbed by the talking bird. She laid one of her thin hands on Ephraim's wrist. "Just like James. And James was the one who sent us to you," she explained, passing him the paper.

"What else did James have to say about Ephraim?"

Cora shook her head. "James said you'd had a tough time with vampires. But he said you could help us. And I believe you can. Please."

I watched, impressed, as Cora used an entirely different sort of compulsion. She placed a hand on Ephraim's shoulder and squeezed slightly. Ephraim smiled, clearly in a state of bliss at being fawned over by a beautiful woman.

"Well, Ephraim *can* help you. Of course. But Ephraim knows what people say about him. Did James tell you Ephraim is insane? Do you believe it, too?" Ephraim asked, suddenly indignant. "Because Ephraim isn't. But the question is, why would Ephraim help you, vampire?"

He swung to face me, his gaze suddenly sharp and probing.

"Far too much blood, too much violence," he continued. "All you care about is satisfying your thirst, and the more you drink, the more you want. A waste of time. Now, witches on the other hand . . . we're a majestic race."

"You are majestic," I said. "And that's why I need your help. I can't take down this vampire alone."

"You want to destroy another vampire? Ephraim needs to hear why." Ephraim gestured in front of him, as if inviting me to take the floor. "If you tell a good story, Ephraim may help you. And if not . . ." Ephraim trailed off ominously.

I looked into his beady eyes. "I am Stefan Salvatore," I said, the name tasting strange on my tongue. I hadn't used my surname since I'd been in England. "And I'm a vampire. I turned twenty years ago because I was young, and stupid, and blindly in love. And I caused destruction. I turned my brother . . . and I killed my father." I heard Cora gasp. I'd never told her how I killed my father. I thought she'd never understand. But now that I was telling my story, I felt compelled to confess all my sins. I had a sense that Ephraim would know if I tried to leave anything out. "I killed men, women, and children. But that's in the past now. I have reformed. I have tried to atone for my early mistakes. I came to England and found work on a farm in Ivinghoe. It was honest, clean work, and for the first time in years I felt I had a purpose. I felt happy."

The word sounded odd even as I said it, but it was true. I had been content with my life in Ivinghoe. "Until I learned about Jack the Ripper and his brutal attacks on women in Whitechapel. I knew it was the work of another vampire, and I suspected it was my brother, so I decided to intervene. The last thing I needed was more blood on my hands."

Ephraim nodded slightly. "This is all a very good, courageous story. I could see it making a nice morality tale to tell children on a dark winter's night. But why are you *here*? And who is this girl?"

"This is Cora. I befriended her sister, Violet, two weeks ago. She had just lost her job and was desperate to find Cora, who was missing. I told Violet I would help her find her sister. I gave Violet shelter, and when things became dangerous, I tried to protect her . . ."

"And yet?" Ephraim urged.

"It didn't work." I shook my head, my voice catching. "Samuel, the vampire I'm after, the true culprit behind the Jack the Ripper murders, attacked her. I hadn't seen it coming. She didn't want to turn into a vampire herself—she chose death. But Samuel found us, killed an innocent boy, and forced her to drink his blood. She turned . . ."

"And now she is not only a vampire, but he has taken her under his wing," Ephraim said. He seemed to know the whole story. I wondered if he *did* know it, and just wanted me to retell it so he could see whether or not I was truthful.

"Yes, he took her. I want to help repair the hurt I've caused and stop Samuel from murdering ever again. Cora just wants to save her sister."

"She's not who you remember anymore," Ephraim said, turning his attention to Cora. "She's a vampire. You're better off without her."

Cora shook her head. "I know what she is. But I still love her. She's my sister. I'll love her no matter what. We just need to get her away from Samuel. I know that if I could only talk to her, I could guide her back to be the kind of vampire Stefan is now."

"And we need some sort of weapon against Samuel, too. He's unaffected by vervain," I explained.

"All right." Ephraim nodded. "Well, the girl's request is easy, but yours will be a bit more difficult. But . . ." he trailed off, squinting at me. His eyes were bright blue and I got the disconcerting feeling that he was looking into my thoughts. "Ephraim will think of something. Your intentions are honorable. Ephraim will help you find your sister and give you a weapon against Samuel. There is no need for money," he said, holding up his hand. "Sometimes, when the money comes into play, the magic gets . . . complicated," he said cryptically. "Ephraim only wants your blood."

"My blood?" I asked, taken aback.

Ephraim laughed maniacally. "And vampires are supposed to be good at hearing. Yes, your blood. It's the fee."

"What will you do with it?" I asked hesitantly.

"You wouldn't understand. Only Ephraim knows its purpose. But the offer is limited, so don't squander Ephraim's magnanimity."

I glanced at Cora. I knew any reason a witch would want a vampire's blood couldn't be good. But we were already in too deep. She bit her lip nervously.

"Ephraim is starting to wonder if he shouldn't take out the vampire in front of him as well."

"I'll give you my blood," I said finally. I put my wrist to my fangs, ready to open my skin.

"Not yet," Ephraim said. He reached into his tattered robe and pulled out a glittering, jewel-encrusted dagger. "When it's time." I nodded, letting my hand drop back to my side.

"First, Ephraim will cast a relocation spell. It's quite simple, but it will do the trick. And no one will get hurt. When the clock strikes three, Violet will appear outside Samuel's home, relocated from wherever she is at the time. She will be alone, but only for a few minutes. Ephraim can't hold everyone off for long."

"So she'll be by herself. And then what?" Cora asked.

"And then you can speak to her. You can try to bring

her with you. You can say good-bye. What you do is up to you. All I can do is facilitate a meeting."

"That's fine," Cora said hastily.

"As for your quest against the Ripper vampire . . ." He paused and rooted through his voluminous pocket before pulling out a handful of thorns, brown and over an inch long.

I reached out to grab them but Ephraim slapped my hand away. "Foolish vampire!" he hissed. "These are very dangerous. This hawthorn is bewitched so that if a vampire touches it, he'll lose strength along with blood. It will block the normal curative powers of human blood."

I nodded, entranced.

"Ephraim will put these in a pouch for you. But be careful," he concluded.

"Thank you," I said sincerely as I carefully took the pouch from Ephraim and tucked it in my pocket.

"And now, time to take some of your blood, vampire." I held out my wrist and watched as Ephraim neatly sliced into my skin. He pulled an ancient vial, crusted with blood, from another pocket and held it up to my wrist, using his fingers to knead and coax drops of blood out of the wound. It was like taking blood from a stone. I was desperately low.

"You need to feed," Ephraim said sagely.

"I will," I said. Or I would once we got back to the ground.

"I think this is enough," he said, holding up the vial to the tiny window. The liquid gleamed in the moonlight, and I watched, entranced. Even though the blood was my own, I was still fascinated by the way it looked. No matter how often I saw it, blood was beautiful.

Ephraim trained his gaze on Cora. "Ephraim needs something from you, too."

"Fine," Cora said proudly, shaking her hair back from her face as she held both her wrists out under his nose.

The raven cawed in protest.

"No, no, no—no blood! What would Ephraim do with human blood? No, your fee is your hair."

"My hair?" Cora asked blankly.

"Just a lock. It helps with the relocation spell. You're her kin."

"All right," Cora said, not flinching as the knife came down dangerously close to her ear. Ephraim took the lock of hair and lit a candle.

"By the burning of this hair
Clear the way to Samuel's lair.
For good or evil may it be,
But let this spell bring her to thee."

He brought the lock of hair to the flame and it exploded in a sphere of purple light. At the center of the orb was an image of Violet under a gaslight, her fangs buried deep in the neck of a well-dressed gentleman.

I shivered. All too quickly, the orb disappeared, plunging the room into darkness.

"You're done here." Ephraim nodded, and the raven cawed.

"Three o'clock, then?" Cora asked.

"Yes. Tell James that Ephraim sends his regards. Goodbye, vampire," Ephraim said, as he swung the vial of blood back and forth.

Cora and I clambered back down the stairs, glad to be leaving Ephraim's oddness behind us. As we stepped out of the tower into the night, I heard the clock strike one long, plaintive stroke: one o'clock. Only a few more hours until we saw Violet.

"You need to eat," Cora reminded me.

"I will," I said. Or I would once we'd set up camp outside Samuel's house. I didn't want something as minor as my diet to waylay our plans.

"Do you want my blood?" Cora asked shyly, holding out her pale arms. The moonlight cast a shaft of light over her skin and I could see blue veins crisscrossing just beneath the surface. I imagined what her blood would taste like. Back when I'd first become a vampire, I couldn't pass a woman without envisioning her blood running down my throat. Then, I'd plan my attack, and feed. Never had a woman offered her blood to me.

I shook my head. "I'll have a pigeon," I decided. "Or a squirrel."

Cora opened her mouth as if she were about to protest. "Fine," she said. "Then let's go hunting."

16

wo hours later, we were waiting outside the gates of Samuel's fashionable Bloomsbury house. Earlier, we'd gone up to Hampstead Heath, where Cora said there was always wildlife. She was a good hunter, with sharp eyes, and she'd pointed out squirrels and rabbits that had zigzagged their way across the grass, But I'd seen the fox, its green eyes unblinking and curious deep in the forest. Cora sat by my side as I drank, just as I sat by her side as she ate buns from the bakery.

It wasn't odd. In fact, it was rather nice.

Now, we sat waiting for Violet. We'd been here for the last hour, not wanting to risk being even a second late. Neither of us talked, and the silence was heavy with anticipation. It felt like the clock had struck two an eternity ago, but I'd lost all sense of time. Cora shivered slightly beside me. Despite the cold, Samuel's lawn was springy and bright. While the rest of the city seemed decrepit, as though it was decaying along with the leaves that fluttered to the cobblestones, the grounds of Lansdowne House seemed fresh. I wondered if this, too, was an enchantment.

Cora kept her gaze fixed on the main entrance of the house.

"Violet may not be the Violet you remember, but that doesn't mean the real Violet isn't somewhere, deep inside," I said, breaking the silence. "It just might take a while to bring her out. When I first became a vampire, I don't know if I'd have listened to a human. Be prepared for anything."

Cora nodded. "I know. But it's different with me and Violet. We're more than close. It's like we share a mind. And even if she's a vampire now, it won't change things. I won't let it," she said, her jaw jutting out determinedly.

You might not have a choice, I thought, but didn't say it aloud. I'd already said enough. And maybe Cora was right. More and more with Cora, I found myself acting like Lexi: the older and world-weary mentor who wanted to show the protégé how it was done. But Cora wasn't my protégé, and she didn't *want* to be anything like me. Besides, maybe things wouldn't change between Cora and Violet. Maybe Damon and I were the monstrous aberrations, the brothers who lost their bond along with their souls. Maybe *Cora*, not me, was Violet's best hope for learning to live a moral life as a vampire. Maybe . . .

Just then, far off in the distance, I heard Big Ben. *One . . . two . . . three.*

"It's time," Cora said, grabbing my hand and digging her fingernails into my skin so deeply that I inhaled sharply. Cora's grip showed what her demeanor hadn't: She was just as nervous as I was that Violet might not be the sister she knew and loved.

A hush descended over us—even the crickets or squirrels we'd heard moments earlier had gone silent. It was as if we were underneath a protective dome, where no one would hear or see what occurred.

Violet staggered through the gates, her face covered with blood and her breathing ragged, as though she'd been running. She was wearing a dark red dress that buttoned up to her chin, but her forearms were bare. Her eyes were glittering in the darkness, and she'd lost the scared, haunted look she'd had as a human.

"Violet!" Cora whispered from the bushes.

Violet paused midstep and glanced over. She looked so confused, it was all I could do not to leap from the bushes, wrap her in my arms, and bring her to safety.

"Violet!" Cora called again.

Violet finally located the source of the voice. Disoriented and defensive, she lunged for Cora, pinning her to the ground. Cora's surprised cry pierced the air.

I plucked Violet off her sister and stood her up to face me. It was clear she was strong, very strong, from her recent feeding. I could hear the steady thrum of blood in her veins. I wondered how many victims she'd already claimed and hoped it was not as many as I had on my conscience.

Violet blinked and tried to focus, her savage grimace melting back to a look of confusion.

"Why . . . Stefan?" she said, shaking her head as if unsure whether she was in a dream. Just for a split second, I saw a glimmer of Violet as I'd known her: a naïve, innocent girl trying to make sense of the world. She turned to her sister. "And Cora?" she asked, as if she could scarcely believe her eyes. "What are you doing here?"

"Oh, Violet. You're alive," Cora said, leaping up and showering her sister with kisses. "I am so sorry. I'm sorry I went away, and I'm sorry for everything. Please forgive me. I never should have left you alone in the first place. Do you forgive me?"

Violet's eyes glittered in the moonlight. She reached out and stroked her sister's cheek. "Of course I forgive you," she said. "Oh, I'm so happy to see you." She drew Cora into an embrace.

Cora hugged her sister hard. "I needed to see you," she said finally. "Stefan and I have been so worried about you."

"You shouldn't be," Violet said in a dulcet voice. "I've been happier than I could ever have imagined. Jewels, furs, parties . . . it's the world we always imagined," she said, twirling a lock of her hair around her index finger. "And it can be yours, too. It'll only take a second, and then you can be just like me. You can say good-bye to dull, dirty London forever. You'll never have to sleep in a tunnel or in a crowded rooming house. It will be my gift to you," Violet said as she lunged toward her sister. I ran toward them and pushed Violet to the ground, holding her there as she writhed and gnashed her fangs. Her face turned into a mask of hatred as she blinked up at me.

"You ruin *everything*, Stefan," she snarled, pushing me away.

"I'm *fixing* everything. And Cora doesn't want to be a vampire. That's not the answer. We've come to take you with us," I explained. "Where you'll be safe."

"Safe?" Violet spat as she stood. "I'm safe here. With Samuel. And I'm happy, too, Stefan. No thanks to you." She sounded like she was issuing a challenge. Her voice had lost all traces of her Irish accent, and was as cold and hard as iron.

"You'll be happier with your sister. You two are family. You don't need Samuel."

"What do you know about what I need?" Violet shot back, hatred dripping from her voice. "You told me not to become a vampire. You told me it would be lonely and terrible. 'A fate worse than death,' was what you said. But you just didn't want me to have any fun. Not like Samuel does." Violet laughed, an icy, tinkling sound. "I pity you. And luckily, I don't have to deal with you. You'll be dead soon enough. Until then, keep away from my sister. She doesn't need your *protection*."

At this, Violet turned to her sister possessively. "Look at you, Cora," she said. "Why, you're a mess. You need me to take care of you."

"No, Violet, come with us. Please, this isn't you," Cora implored.

"Oh, Cora," Violet said, grasping her sister's hands in hers. "Don't you see? I have everything I've ever wanted. Join me. It could be just like we talked about, me and you, taking on the world!"

"Don't listen to her!" I interjected.

Violet turned and glared at me. "You're the one who's been lying. She needs a real vampire to protect her. And to think I believed you were so brave and so strong. You're nothing like Samuel. You're nothing at all," she hissed.

Her words sliced through my stomach. There was nothing left of the girl I'd kissed on the hill in Ivinghoe.

"Violet, *please*. You're hurting me," Cora said, twisting her hands in Violet's grip. "Stefan—"

"Shh," Violet said tenderly, brushing her lips across

Cora's forehead. "I'm here now. He doesn't matter. He's nothing to you."

"You don't know what you're doing, Violet," I said, lunging toward her. But Violet stepped daintily out of reach, still holding Cora tight.

"And you do?" Violet laughed sharply. "Good-bye, Stefan. I'll send Samuel out to deal with you." She dragged Cora across the lawn as Cora tried desperately to claw her way out of her sister's grasp.

"Let go, Violet!" Cora yelled futilely. "Stop!"

I barreled toward them and knocked Violet away from Cora. But Violet quickly retaliated with a kick that sent me flying into the wall of Lansdowne House. In the split second it took me to regain my feet, Violet snatched Cora, threw her over her shoulder, and sped over the threshold into house.

The door clicked closed. I rushed against it, but it wouldn't budge. All I could hear was the faint sound of Violet's laughter from within.

Down at my feet, I noticed a glint of silver. Cora's vervain necklace. She was defenseless against her bloodthirsty sister, and Samuel's compulsion.

She was doomed.

17

I circled around, hoping to find some entry into the house. I knew it was no use—I hadn't been invited in—but I couldn't give up on Cora yet. At one rear window, I caught sight of Violet leading Cora up a curved staircase. I rapped desperately on the glass, not caring that Violet would hear me as well.

Both girls whirled around.

"I'll be back," I mouthed to Cora. Her eyes were huge and her face was twisted with fright. I didn't think Violet would kill her, but beyond that, I had no idea what would happen. Would Violet turn her? Compel her?

I had to rescue Cora as soon as possible.

Without a second thought, I began to run, my feet thudding against the cobblestones, heading toward Whitechapel and James at vampire speed. I didn't care who saw me. I didn't care about anything. All I wanted was to move, to hear the blood coursing through my veins, to see the spots of light in front of my eyes that signaled I was close to fainting. To know I was doing everything in my power to save her.

I turned down the twisty alleyway and burst into James's store, not bothering to knock.

"James!" I called, my voice taking on a hysterical tone. "James!"

He shuffled out from the back of the store, clad in a white nightshirt and holding a candle in front of him. From his expression, I could tell he wasn't entirely surprised to see me.

"Hello," he said, using the candle to light a candelabra at the front of the store. "What can I do for you?"

"Cora's gone. Violet took her," I said dully. "Damon's disappeared. Samuel's getting away with murder every night, and a crazy witch is now running around with a vial of my blood. I don't have any money, my name is worthless, and for all I know the relocation spell was cast for Violet's benefit."

James looked up at me, grimacing. "You're ranting like a madman," he said.

"I'm sorry. But I'm in a hurry. I need to get Cora back before anything horrible happens to her. Do you understand?" I asked firmly. I didn't trust James. I didn't trust anyone. My gaze landed on the beating hearts in a jar on a shelf. What did those do? I had a wild desire to buy everything in the store. The answer had to be somewhere. And I was feeling more and more that the hawthorn in my pocket was useless, just a ruse to get my blood.

"Sit down." James gestured at a threadbare red chair across from me. Realizing how tired I was, I sank down, massaging my temples. Mice were scurrying in the far corners of the store, and it was impossible to tell whether they were there because it was filthy or because they were an essential part of the inventory.

Across the counter, James was bustling around at his small stove range. Finally, he turned to me, a steaming mug of tea in his hands. "Goat's blood. It'll cure what ails you."

Of course. Why had I expected anything else? "It won't," I said angrily. "I just don't understand what I can do. I tried magic, I tried force, I have these *supposedly* bewitched thorns . . ."

"Hawthorns?" James perked up.

I nodded.

"Well, that's a good weapon."

"It is?" I asked in disbelief.

"Yes. And there's your problem. Ephraim handed you a weapon that might actually work against your enemy, and you shove it away because you don't trust the source.

And therein lies the rub. You may be immortal, have the strength of ten lions, and be as quick as lightning, but you need to accept help. You can't fight Samuel alone."

It didn't take long for me to grasp what James was implying. "I need Damon."

"Good." James nodded, as though I were an exceptionally clever student. "He's at a boardinghouse over on Brushfield Street. Two blocks to the west. Came in four times yesterday and nearly cleaned me out of my vampire-hunting supplies. He got a holed stone to see the future, he stocked up on a few stakes, he got some hazel arrows for a crossbow, even though hazel is more effective in subduing bad *fairies* . . . I'm telling you, I'm making a killing off him." I winced at the phrase. "Sorry," James said. "Go find your brother. Maybe he'll give you some fresh ideas. At the very least, it'll keep you off the streets. No good can come from ranting and raving like a lunatic, mark my words."

"Thanks," I said stiffly. I stood up, feeling awkward. Did James just feel sorry for me, a vampire who couldn't stomach death? Or was James a true friend in the vast network of underworld creatures, one who hadn't lost his humanity? "Truly, thank you," I said again, searching my pocket for some token with which to repay him.

"No need," James said airily. "You'll pay me back in some way. In the future."

With a parting glance, I left, following James's directions

to the boardinghouse, my heart thudding against my chest. I tried not to think about what Violet was doing with Cora, not allowing my imagination to go to the dark places that probably held the truth.

I stopped at a tall brick building with a ROOMS FOR RENT sign hanging in its entryway and knocked on the door.

"Come in. Door's open," a voice croaked. I pushed open the door. A wizened old man was sitting at a rickety desk, poring over a ledger book. I coughed. "I'm looking for . . . Damon de Croix," I said as he looked up.

"Damon de Croix?" The man let out a harsh bark. "If you mean the half-crazed gentleman who paid me with a handful of foreign currency, then he's in Room 411. Although God knows what he's doing in there. By the stench of it, he's a failed taxidermist." He wrinkled his nose in disgust.

"Thank you," I said, racing up the stairs to the fourth floor. I slammed against the cheap wood of the door, easily breaking the lock. There, in the filthy, dark room, was Damon, bending over an oversize flowerpot on the windowsill. It was amazing that anything could grow in the weak light coming through the dirty window glass. Out of the corner of my eye, I spotted a wooden crossbow propped against the cast-iron bed.

"Brother," Damon said dully, glancing up from the windowsill, sounding neither surprised nor angry. It was as though he was expecting me. I wondered if James had given him an identical message. He may not have been a witch, but if James could get Damon and me to reconcile, then he certainly worked magic.

"What are you doing?" I asked. It was hard to concentrate with the scent of vervain everywhere. I imagined that was what was growing in the pots. I felt woozy and weak, and I wondered why Damon was inflicting this torture on himself.

"I'm dosing myself with vervain," Damon explained. "If Samuel can do it, I can, too. And then, once I'm fully immune, I'll dose the water supply. Prevent Samuel from feeding and compelling in this city. The details are fuzzy, but the plan will work."

"You're ingesting vervain?" I asked in disbelief as I looked at the six paltry vervain plants. All they were doing was torturing my brother.

"Sometimes, brother," Damon began, rolling his eyes, "you need to understand an enemy to vanquish him. Plus, suffering only makes you stronger," he said resolutely.

I took a seat on the bed. I hadn't come here to fight. I needed help. But what I wanted was the in-charge, confident Damon, not the rambling, maniacal man in front of me. Despite his outburst on the night of the Ripper killings, I knew he cared about Cora. I only hoped the mention of her would bring him to his senses.

"Samuel has Cora."

Damon stiffened and dropped a sprig of vervain to the ground. But then he shrugged. "Well, we knew that would happen, eventually, didn't we?" he said bitterly.

"I need to get her back," I said firmly. "And I need your help."

"You need my help," he mocked. "What about all the other times you've said that? Didn't work out so well." He stood and crossed over to me, so close that I could smell blood on his breath. The rich, smoky scent was obviously human, and I couldn't help but wonder where his blood supply was coming from.

"You need my help, too," I said firmly. "Like it or not, we're in this together. And we need to fight together, not *against* one another. We're on the same side." The desperation in my voice was plain, and I was showing all my cards. I didn't have a strategy, and I wasn't trying to one-up him.

A flicker of something—doubt, anger, or acceptance, I wasn't sure—crossed Damon's face.

"All right," he said finally. "I'll help you. But this time, brother, we do it my way. You follow my directions in the fight. I've been doing research," he said, gesturing to piles of musty books piled on the floor. Damon? Doing research? This was a side of him I'd never seen. He'd never been one for books, always preferring to trust his instincts. "I have everything. Wooden bullets, sand, stakes . . ."

"Sand?" I asked in confusion.

Damon shrugged. "Apparently it's a deterrent. It wasn't for me when I was in the Sahara, but James said it could slow down a vampire on the run. I figure it can't hurt." He paused. "In the end, Samuel will be destroyed. It will be bloody, and there may be unintended victims. If you can't handle that, then get out now and leave me to do what needs to be done."

"I'm all in," I said calmly. "And Damon . . . I'm sorry."

Damon nodded. "All right," he said. In Damon's vocabulary, "all right" was as good as "apology accepted." I decided I'd take it. I had to.

"Samuel has an office in the Magdalene Asylum where he feeds on the girls and keeps some of his campaign papers. We can sneak in, wait for him, and then . . ." Damon trailed off. Then what? Kill him? Follow him? Beg for Cora's life back? This was going to be tricky, and we couldn't afford to make any mistakes.

"It's almost daylight. The girls will be going to Mass soon. We'll sneak in then," I said. "We can set traps with our supplies. If this is what we're doing, we have to go now."

"I have weapons," Damon muttered. "I've been experimenting with explosives. Of course, I'd love to kill Samuel with my bare hands, but I wouldn't mind watching his body burn."

"Great," I said. I was glad we were agreeing on

something, even if it was the best way to murder our mutual enemy.

"Let's kill him. I want blood on the floor, and his body ripped apart. I want him destroyed," Damon said as if in a trance. His eyes were bloodshot and his skin was pale. The porter at the door had been right—anyone would take him for a madman.

He was out for blood. I was out to save Cora. But for now, our mission was the same: Take down Samuel in any way possible.

18

The sun was just coming over the horizon when we reached the Magdalene Asylum. Damon had an oversize rucksack on his back, in which he'd pack his explosives, his crossbow, his stakes, and my tiny pouch of hawthorn.

When we reached the Asylum, it was nearly seven. Our plan was to wait until the girls left to go to Mass, then sneak through the back and find the office Cora had described. We'd set our traps in the office, lie in wait, and then, when Samuel came in, we'd attack.

The church bells pealed and, as if on cue, the doors burst open and a line of girls trailed out behind Sister Benedict. I recognized several of them from the benefit. Their eyes darted from left to right, as if they were afraid Jack the Ripper would attack them at any moment. It was clear they were shaken by Cathy's murder, but I doubted they remembered the incident in the basement at the benefit. Samuel would have made sure of that. I wondered if they thought Cora had met the same fate.

As soon as the line of girls turned the street corner, my brother and I looked at each other.

"It's time," Damon said tersely. We stole to the rear of the brick building and found a small, unused door that led to the basement. Damon pushed against it with his shoulder, and it burst open.

"Shhh!" I said, too late, as it banged against the wall. The iron-rich smell of blood wafted toward us from the passageway.

Together, we tiptoed down a set of rickety wooden steps and into the basement of the Asylum. The light streaming from a few tiny windows gave the hallway a grayish glow. A row of nondescript doors with glass windows lined the hallway. One of them must be Samuel's office. I cocked my head, but I couldn't make out any noise except for the dripping of water in the laundry at the end of the hall.

We crept closer, following each other's movements in silence.

"Wait," Damon whispered. He paused and rifled through the bag, finally pulling out a crossbow and a stake. He passed the stake over to me. "Just in case," he said as he propped it on his shoulder.

We continued to creep down the hall until the sound of footsteps stopped our progress.

"Get ready!" Damon hissed.

What if it was one of the nuns or one of the girls? The last thing I wanted was for them to see the de Croix brothers creeping around the basement brandishing weapons. I hid the stake under my shirt, ready if I needed it, but hidden, just in case. Damon kept the crossbow raised, but sunk deeper into the shadows of the basement.

Just then, a large figure lumbered into view. He was wearing filthy clothes and looked like a giant in the cramped basement.

"Who are you?" he asked gruffly. He had grease stains on his clothes, and I wondered if he was a handyman for the Asylum.

"From the Magdalene Church," I said. "Sister Agatha's asked me to check on the building. There's been a lot of structural damage due to rain. Want to make sure it won't collapse," I lied.

"All right," the man said, scratching his head.

"I'm surprised Sister Agatha didn't mention anything."

"No, she didn't tell me," the man parroted. He was so tentative in his words and actions I thought he must be slow, and was relieved when he shuffled on down the hall.

Damon moved out of the shadows, shaking his head. "What was that idiot doing down here?"

"It was just an Asylum worker," I said, hoping I was right.

"If he comes back, I'll kill him," Damon decided. "We can't take any more chances." He shot me a glance as though he expected me to disagree, but I nodded. He was right.

"Good," Damon said.

We started up the hallway, trying the doors on either side as we passed. The fifth door led us into Samuel's office. Damon glanced at me, triumphant. "Let's get to work," he said, rifling through his bag. He pulled out a pair of gloves and tossed them to me.

I pulled them on, then set about tying hawthorn needles dipped in vervain to a length of wire and stringing it around the office. Damon stood on a chair in the corner, rigging a gun loaded with wooden bullets to be triggered by the trip wire now lining the room.

We worked silently. Damon had been right—it was him or us. The traps were crude and makeshift, but I hoped they would be enough. They had to be.

Searching for anything else we could use against Samuel, I opened a drawer stuffed with yellowed papers. I rifled through them, glanced at the dates: *1888*, *1865*, *1780*. Samuel clearly had at least a century on us. I wondered when and how he had been turned.

Just as I was about to put the papers back in the drawer,

I spotted the word *Atlanta* in the old-fashioned, slanting script.

"Damon!" I hissed. He carefully picked his way around the traps. When he'd reached my side, I pointed to the date on the document in my hand: *1864.*

"What is this?" Damon whispered roughly, clawing the letter out of my hands.

"Give it back," I said.

Damon shook his head, holding the letter out of my grasp. He scanned it quickly, then sighed in despair. "It's not from her," he said, handing it back.

> *Dear Sir,*
> *This is to inform you that your letter, received in Atlanta and addressed to a Miss Katherine Pierce, is being returned as undeliverable. The address listed was destroyed under Sherman's siege, with no survivors.*

It was signed by someone I could only assume was a long-dead postal clerk.

"Do you think she was trying to escape him?" I asked.

"She must have been," Damon said, his mouth set in a tight line.

I nodded. In truth, who knew what Katherine and Samuel's relationship had been? They were the only two who knew for sure, and Katherine was dead—and Samuel would be, imminently. But from the way Damon's shoulders relaxed, I knew he needed to believe that what Samuel and Katherine had wasn't a true love.

I pulled more papers from the drawer. While Damon was focused on our upcoming battle, I was intent on finding out more about Samuel. I knew it didn't matter; he'd be dead in hours.

And then I saw it.

The paper was yellow and crumbling, but five words at the bottom said everything we needed to know.

> *With eternal love,*
> *Your Katherine.*

My eyes followed Damon as he double-checked our traps. He couldn't know. I had saved my brother's life several times since we reunited in London, but what I did next was perhaps the most I'd ever done to protect him. I took the paper and ripped it into dozens of pieces, letting them fall to the stone floor like snow.

Damon would spend eternity thinking Katherine had loved him. He couldn't survive otherwise.

Several hours later, as Damon and I crouched in Samuel's office, I was still thinking about Katherine. There hadn't been any more letters from Katherine hidden in the desk, and I wondered if Samuel had deliberately destroyed or hidden Katherine's other letters. I wondered when Katherine and Samuel had met, and how many decades they'd spent discovering every secret of their bodies and brains. I'd only known Katherine for several weeks, and her image was branded indelibly in my mind. What could it possibly have been like to know her for generations?

Just then, I heard a loud bang, different than the sounds we'd been listening to all day, of girls hurrying to and from the laundry room, of nuns clicking their rosary beads as they walked by, of the building settling into itself. This sounded like a clap of thunder.

"I'm going to investigate," I said, stepping delicately over our cobweb of traps. Maybe it was time for us to move into our hiding spot—the tiny coat closet in the corner of the room—and wait for Samuel to enter.

I cracked open the door, peering into the hallway. It was empty. The nuns and the girls must have been well trained not to go near Samuel's office. Except for the odd interaction we'd had with the handyman in the morning, we'd barely heard footsteps. I stepped out, but saw nothing that could've produced the noise. I was about to turn back, when I thought I saw movement in one of the other rooms.

"Damon!" I hissed, before creeping to the window and

peering in. I blinked in surprise. There was Cora, alone and unprotected. She was sitting in the corner with her knees hugged to her chest. "Damon, it's Cora!"

I pushed the door with all my might and heard the lock break, but the door itself barely cracked open.

Cora looked up in fear when she heard the commotion.

"It's me, Stefan," I whispered through the slim opening. Relief was evident on her face, and then I heard the clanking of chains. Cora was shackled to the wall, and it was impossible for her to stand completely upright. "I'm coming!" I hurled my weight against the door again.

"Violet brought me here," Cora said miserably. "She brought me around the back, where a man took me and chained me up."

"Stay there!" I instructed. "Damon, help get the door open. It's just jammed," I lied to Cora. I could sense something was holding the door shut. It wasn't a lock—my vampire strength could pull through that. It was something stronger, more sinister. My stomach knotted as Damon joined me and we both shoved against the door with our hands. Still, it wouldn't budge wider than a half inch.

"What's wrong?" I asked Damon. No simple door should be a match for the two of us, even with my diet of animal blood.

Damon shook his head and picked up his crossbow. "I don't know. We'll help her later. He'll be back soon."

"Stefan, go. Help your brother," Cora said, sliding back to the filthy floor in a heap. "He's right. It won't do any good if Samuel sees anything amiss. I'll be fine."

I gave Cora an encouraging smile before Damon and I retreated back into Samuel's office. We jammed our bodies into the coat closet, not daring to speak. Damon had the crossbow at the ready. We weren't particularly well hidden, and I knew we only had seconds to react when Samuel finally entered. The waiting was agony—and I could only imagine how hard it was for Cora. Who knew what torture she'd endured?

Suddenly, I heard someone whistling discordantly in the hallway. Damon glanced at me and nodded. Samuel was here.

The door clicked open. I braced myself, listening for the twang of the wire as it was tripped, but nothing happened. Instead, Samuel stood absolutely still in the doorway, sniffing the air.

Quick as a flash, he reached into his boot to pull out a stake. Damon used that moment to burst from our hiding spot and release a vervain-soaked bolt from the crossbow. It landed in Samuel's gut, and he fell to the ground in a heap.

I leaped to my feet and raced toward Samuel, careful to avoid the trip wire. He lay on the ground, the crossbow bolt deep in his stomach, his face a mask of rage as he reached to pull it out. Damon appeared by my side, standing over Samuel with a candle in his hand.

"I've been waiting for this," Damon said in a low voice. "And I knew revenge would be mine. I want you to burn before you get to hell," Damon hissed, leaning down and allowing the flame to brush against the sleeve of Samuel's shirt. The flames ripped through the starched white fabric. Samuel writhed in pain, but didn't make a sound. For a second I wondered: Was he impervious to fire, too? But I could see a path of charred flesh where the fire had touched him. It just wasn't enough to destroy him.

"Kill him!" I implored urgently as I rummaged through Damon's rucksack for the hawthorn-tipped stake. I wanted to get Cora out of here as quickly as possible.

"Oh, I will, brother," Damon cackled as I yanked the stake from the bag. "But first, I want to play a little game with Samuel. After all, he seems to love games," Damon said, setting fire to the cuff of Samuel's trouser leg. The flame sparked and danced up the hem of his pants. "Once you're fully ablaze, I'll let all of London know you were the Ripper. I have evidence. I have Cora, who'll testify. I have the other girls from the Asylum. I'll be a hero. And who knows, maybe I'll even be the new London councilor," Damon said, as he lit the other leg on fire.

"Damon, either I'm going to stake him or you will. But

it's time," I said firmly. Damon ignored me and kept placing the candle to Samuel's clothing.

"Damon, I'm going to stake him," I warned, raising my arm high above my head, ready to drive the weapon into Samuel's ancient flesh.

"What, you don't have anything to say? And you were always so talkative," Damon taunted. "Always so *creative*. Coming up with the Jack the Ripper plot, lying about Katherine . . . it's a shame you've reached the end of your story," Damon said, allowing the flame to brush Samuel's neck.

I closed my eyes and, summoning all my strength, I plunged the stake toward Samuel.

All of a sudden, I heard a gunshot, then a shriek. I dropped the hawthorn stake in surprise. On the floor was Henry, a hole from the wooden bullet in his head, his eyes still wide open. Violet was crouched in the doorway, keening. Behind her, Cora stood with her hands to her mouth, looking on in horror.

Damon's attention turned to Henry, a slight smile of satisfaction on his lips. Samuel was rolling around the ground, desperately trying to extinguish the flames consuming his body. "Kill him!" I yelled again as I picked up the stake and rushed toward Henry. If he wasn't dead yet, he would be in seconds. I felt a searing sensation on my ankle—the hawthorn trip wire. Pain ran up my leg and through my body until it flooded my brain. The room swam in front of me.

"Cora!" I yelled. "Run!"

Cora took a step back. And that was when I saw it: two holes in her neck, as round and neat as shodding nails, still oozing blood. Could Violet have fed on her own sister?

"Run!" I yelled again, my voice ragged. I couldn't have her standing near this room, amid traps that could go off at any moment. Whatever happened tonight, one thing was certain: Cora could not die.

Cora took off down the hallway, away from the fight. I stood above Henry, ready to stake him, when someone grabbed my shoulders from behind and flung me against the far wall. Violet leapt across the room and tried to wrestle me to the floor.

Having just fed, she was strong, but my age made me stronger. I pushed her back, pinning her to the floor. I watched in disgust as she writhed. How could she drink from her own sister? I may have turned Damon into a vampire, but I'd never hurt him intentionally. I just wanted us to be together, forever. Violet seemed to have lost any moral compass.

"Violet," I whispered urgently, my face inches from hers. I remembered how in Ivinghoe, the only thing she had wanted was to die with a kiss. I wished that I could kiss her now and wake her from this nightmare, but I couldn't. She was too far gone. All I could do was subdue her, and give Damon time to finish off Samuel and Henry. Our traps had served their purpose, and we'd severely wounded them both. Now all we had to do was use their weakness to our advantage.

"You hurt my brother, you answer to me!" Samuel's voice jolted my attention away. The flames had gone out and although his skin was charred, he was already starting to heal. Samuel held Damon by his throat so tight that I knew one flick of his wrist could snap Damon's neck. Sensing my distraction, Violet clawed at me, catching me off guard and flipping me onto my back.

I struggled to break free of Violet's grip. She was coursing with energy. I twisted, trying to free myself. There was no way Damon could hold his own against Samuel if he was at his full strength. I needed to help him. But Violet merely laughed at my attempts to escape.

"Violet, please," I said, grabbing her hands and staring into her eyes. "I know you. You're not like them. Come with us. Fight with us." But even as I said it, I knew it was no good. There was nothing but hatred in her eyes.

"Samuel," she called sharply. "I need a stake."

Meanwhile, I realized with horror that Henry was sitting up. He was rubbing his temple, as though he were merely suffering a migraine.

We might die.

It was the first time I'd actually considered it a concrete possibility. I tried once more to break away. Samuel reached down with his free hand and picked one of Damon's many pointed stakes off the floor.

"For you, my pet," Samuel said, tossing it to Violet. "Do me proud."

"I tried to save you," I said, in a last, desperate attempt to get through to her. "You don't owe me friendship, but if you kill me, you'll regret it."

"She won't," Samuel said, smiling. Now that his brother was none the worse for the wear and Damon and I were entirely at his mercy, he had no reason not to be happy. "In fact, I think she'll look back on this as the day she truly came into her own."

I kicked the air, my foot hitting Samuel in the shin. "Impudent," he said, scowling down at me. "Both of you. You're dying twenty years too late."

Violet was deadly serious as she pulled the stake back. Her elbow was steady, and I felt a tremor of fear in my heart. Was this it?

"Think about what you're doing," I hissed through clenched teeth. "You went to the dark side. But you still have a choice. If you kill me, you'll remember it for eternity. And trust me, you won't be able to handle it. It will destroy you."

For a fraction of a second, she seemed to hesitate.

Summoning all my strength, I pushed her away, wrenching the stake from her hand and pinning her to the floor. I knew I had to push the stake deep into Violet's heart now. She was too far gone, a lost cause. This was the only mercy I could give her.

But before I could strike, Henry blindsided me, knocking me sideways. He pushed my back against the wall, smiling and cackling maniacally.

"We meet again, Stefan," he said. "I think, with our history, it's only fair I kill you, not Violet. Don't you agree?" I kicked at him, trying to escape.

"Damon, kill Henry!" I hissed urgently. In a rush of adrenaline and strength, Damon broke free from Samuel's grasp, twisting Samuel's wrist almost clear around in the process. Samuel staggered back in pain as his bones started to right themselves. Damon took those brief moments to rush over, a candle clutched in his hand. Without hesitation, Damon brought the candle down to Henry's shirt. Already weakened from his previous brush with death, the flame took to his damaged flesh immediately, igniting him like a human torch. He stumbled back, trying to put out the fire that was steadily engulfing him.

"Get Cora!" Damon yelled sharply. "They might have accomplices!" I pushed past Henry and raced into the hallway, grabbing Cora and pulling her close to me. Now everyone, including Samuel and Violet, stood staring in horror at Henry. The flames were consuming him, seeming to grow exponentially with each of his pained cries.

"Help him!" Samuel shrieked, pushing Violet toward the flames, but it was too late. Henry fell to the ground, motionless, his body completely ablaze. Samuel must have known he was gone. I heard Damon's long, low chuckle.

Samuel's face contorted with grief and rage. He lunged at Damon, tackling him to the ground, and pulled the crossbow bolt from his abdomen. With a scream, he stabbed Damon in the chest. Cora clung to me while Violet approached Samuel and placed a tentative hand on his shoulder. He shrugged her off.

Before I could move, Samuel slung Damon over his shoulder and stalked past me. Damon was still breathing, but he was gravely injured.

In the hallway, Samuel turned.

"Because of you two, Henry is dead," he said, each word slick with rage. His eyes were hollow and bloodshot, and each word sounded like a curse. "Your brother will suffer for this. And then he will die," Samuel said, as though relaying a prophecy. "Mark my words." He pulled one of the hawthorns off the wire and plunged it into my chest just an inch from my heart.

"*Stake him*," Damon whispered, barely conscious. I grasped wildly for the stake Violet had dropped, struggling as I felt the effects of the hawthorn course through my veins.

But by the time I had the stake in my hand, Samuel was gone, with Damon and Violet in his grasp. I sank to the ground, left with Cora's cries and the acrid stench of Henry's burned body. In the distance, I heard Samuel release a ragged wail, mourning for his brother.

We were in this battle to the death. Either Damon and I would live, or Samuel would finish us both. There was no other option. Either he'd join Henry in hell, or we would.

I didn't know how the next battle would play out. All I knew was that I had to get my brother back.

EPILOGUE

I'd spent the last twenty years on the run, always wishing I could stay in one place. Now, I was bound to London, the dark, dank city where blood ran into the Thames and creatures of the night made their home in its monuments. I was bound to Cora, to Samuel, and to a complex web of deceit, blood, and threats. We were all entangled until one of us—be it by strength or spells or intelligence—broke free.

And most of all, I was bound to Damon. But it was about more than brotherly bonds. Now, it was truly the age-old battle between good and evil. Except it wasn't that simple. Because all of us had sins that could never be undone.

This wasn't a battle to be won by force. This

was a battle to be won by intelligence, by Power, and—I realized more and more, as my mind kept returning to the impossibly blocked door in the Asylum—magic.

No rules. No limits. The only certainty was death.

There was a moment after Samuel dragged an injured Damon away when it seemed as though my spirit had left my body. It was how I'd felt when a bullet from my father's gun pierced my chest all those years ago in Mystic Falls: a split-second of agony, followed by a blankness that radiated from the very core of my being.

A low-pitched moan echoed off the stone walls and caused my mind and my soul to snap back to the damp basement of the Magdalene Asylum, where our battle had come to its horrible end only moments before. The smell of Henry's burning flesh still clung to the room. There was blood pooled on the floor and spattered against the wall, as though the subterranean office had become an impromptu butcher shop. Which, I suppose, it had.

Standing in the corner, Cora moaned again, her hand clasped to her mouth. Cora was an innocent girl caught in a nightmare from which there was no waking. Only a fortnight ago, Samuel had turned her sister, Violet, into a vampire. Ever since then, Cora had been doing anything she could to try to save her, including infiltrating the Magdalene Asylum, of which Samuel was a well-known benefactor. We had hoped to get closer to Samuel, to discover his weaknesses, anything that could help us understand his relentless vendetta against us. Because the murders weren't committed for the blood. As vampires, we could kill quickly and cleanly if necessary—but we didn't need to kill for blood. Samuel especially didn't: As a benefactor to the Magdalene Asylum, he'd been able to drink his fill from its residents, compelling them to offer their necks to him, and then forget all about the encounter. So why was Samuel intent on brutally slaying and slicing open his victims? It didn't make sense.

In the process of our investigation, we'd lost Damon. And Cora was losing hope. Cora had desperately wanted to believe her sister could maintain her humanity. But that wasn't to be the case. Not only had Violet fought brutally against Damon and me moments earlier, but she'd hurt and fed off of Cora. I could only imagine the horrors Cora was reliving as she stood in the corner.

But I couldn't think of what had happened. I needed

to think of the future—and I needed to save Damon.

"We can't stay here. Let's go home." I punched my hand through a window, leaving a trail of blood as shards of glass fell to the floor. I grabbed Cora by the waist and effortlessly pulled her through the window, and together, the two of us raced from the Magdalene Asylum gates and out onto the rain-slicked streets of London. Our destination was the Underground tunnel where we'd spent our nights for the last week.

High above us, a few fireworks lit the night sky, and I remembered it was the evening before Guy Fawkes Day, the holiday during which the British celebrated victory over treason. Groups of drunken revelers roamed the streets with torches, singing songs as they rejoiced. A drunken man wavered by, singing, a pint of ale clutched unsteadily in one hand, and I caught one of the lyrics:

Last Guy Fawkes Day as I hear say,
The Devil about did roam.

I grimaced. Little did he know how apt his off-key drinking song was at describing the current situation in London. The sound of my footsteps echoed in my ears, and I could hear Cora's blood thumping double-time in her veins. I knew from the papers that policemen were hiding in every shadowy alley, on the lookout for the Ripper. I ran at vampire speed past them, pulling Cora with me, and they were oblivious to our presence.

Of course, the police presence was useless. While they were shivering on the streets, on guard for the Ripper's next attack, the murderer was comfortably ensconced at home in Lansdowne House, most likely plotting ways to destroy my brother.

I couldn't help but wonder whether Samuel was torturing Damon the way Damon had eventually killed Henry. Damon had stopped at nothing, including burning Henry's skin with a torch, to make him suffer. Had Samuel somehow upped the ante? Or had he simply slain him with a stake and thrown his lifeless body in the Thames? Torture or kill? It was a lose-lose situation, but I found myself hoping for torture as I pulled Cora around the corner toward the tunnel opening.

We were home. No one was chasing us. No one seemed to be here, perhaps put off by the signs that surrounded the work area, all clearly stating that trespassing was strictly prohibited by the Metropolitan Police.

I jumped down the opening, unfazed by the drop to the bottom of the tunnel. That was one of the advantages of being a vampire: I always knew I'd land on my feet.

I helped Cora down and the two of us faced each other. Despite the darkness, I could see everything, from the packed dirt walls to the pebbles scattered on the ground.

Meanwhile, Cora blinked several times, her eyes adjusting to the lack of light.

Suddenly, a creature darted past our feet. It was a rat, almost the size of a small cat. Cora's eyes widened and I expected her to scramble away in surprise. But instead, she grabbed a large stone from the tunnel floor and threw it at the creature. The scuffling stopped.

Cora bent down, scooped up the dead rodent, and held it out to me.

"You need to eat," she urged. The rat's head hung limply off Cora's palm.

"Thank you." I placed my mouth to its fur before piercing the thin skin with my fangs. The whole time, I was aware of Cora's unflinching gaze. But what did it matter? It wasn't like my drinking blood was a surprise to her. She'd seen me bare my fangs to feed, she'd seen me battle Henry and Samuel. The liquid tasted bitter and oily, and yet I felt it calm my body as it ran through my veins.

Once I'd drunk all I could, I threw the carcass to the ground, wiped my mouth with the back of my hand, and smiled tersely at Cora. Our friendship was one I'd never experienced with a human since I'd become a vampire. Even when Callie had discovered my identity back in New Orleans, I never fed in front of her. I hid my fangs and masked my yearnings, wanting her to only see the best in me. But Cora was different.

"Was that enough?" she asked, sliding into a seated position and crossing her legs under her gray dress, now spattered with dirt and blood. Dark shadows surrounded her eyes, and there were smudges of grime on her cheeks. Both made her freckles stand out, as though her skin were a map of a constellation-filled night sky. Her teeth were chattering. It was cold all over London as a languid October had turned into a bitter November. And it was especially frigid in the tunnel, where the walls were beaded with condensation and a misty gray fog swirled around the darkness.

"It was, thank you. How are you?" I asked, feeling stupid as soon as the words escaped my lips. She'd just killed a rodent in the tunnel of an all-but-abandoned construction site for the London Underground. She'd been betrayed by her vampire sister, and was on the run for her life. She'd witnessed friends dying, vampires torturing one another, and bodies burned to ashes. How did I think she'd feel?

"I'm alive," Cora said. "I believe that counts for something." She attempted a laugh, but it came out as a sputtery cough. I patted her on the back and was surprised when she leaned in and gave me a hug. I couldn't imagine why she'd want to get close to me after all she'd seen me do.

"I'm sorry I put you in danger," I said hollowly. "I should have known that we couldn't reason with Violet.

I should never have brought you to see her." Before we'd gone to the Magdalene Asylum for our showdown with Samuel, a witch cast a locator spell to help Cora and I find Violet. When we went to see her, she hadn't listened to anything we'd said and had kidnapped Cora.

"You wouldn't have been able to keep me away from Violet," Cora said firmly. "You told me she wouldn't be the same. But deep down I believed she'd still be my sister. Now I know I was wrong." Cora shuddered. I nodded, encouraging her to continue.

"I was so *stupid*, Stefan," Cora said, her face twisting into a mask of rage. "I thought I could get through to her. I thought she could change. But there was nothing of my sister left in her. She fed off of me, Stefan. She brought me to the Asylum, and asked a man named Seaver, the groundskeeper, to lock me into that room. I tried to escape, but Seaver started chanting, and suddenly, I was completely trapped." Cora's lower lip wobbled as tears spilled down her cheeks. Almost immediately, she wiped them away with the back of her hand and set her mouth in a firm line.

"He must have put a spell on the room," I said slowly. I remembered how small and helpless Cora had looked in that room in the Magdalene Asylum. Even though her arms and legs were free of any chains to bind her, she'd been utterly immobile. She must have been terrified.

"We need to see Ephraim," I decided. The only thing I knew for certain was that if Samuel had witches on his side, he was capable of anything.

"No!" Cora yelped. "Not Ephraim. I had a bad feeling about him. How do we know that Ephraim isn't working for Samuel? If my own flesh and blood turned against me, no one can be trusted," Cora said, setting her jaw. "We need to come up with another plan."

"Ephraim isn't Seaver—he won't hurt you. We need someone who can perform magic on our side. Otherwise, Samuel will have the advantage over us," I said. I stood up and paced back and forth, willing my mind to come up with a smart trap that would ensnare Samuel and free my brother. But I still felt weak and shaky and utterly unable to concentrate. The rat blood had only taken the edge off my hunger.

"I think you should drink real blood," Cora said quietly. "Like your brother. Like Samuel. It would make you strong enough to fight him, right? It would make the fight even, like you said." Her eyes glittered like diamonds in the darkness.

"I can't!" I exploded, unleashing all the tension I'd held during the day as my voice echoed off the walls of the tunnel, sending rodents skittering to unknown hiding spots. "I can't control myself. When Damon feeds, he's smarter and faster. When I feed, all I want is more blood.

I can't think logically or rationally. All I can think of is the next kill. I'm a beast on blood, Cora."

Cora opened her mouth as if to say something, then thought better of it. "All right. But Stefan," she said, grabbing my wrist with a surprisingly strong grip, "this is a war, and I won't have you lose on principle."

"What do you mean?" I yanked my wrist away as I continued to pace up and down the tunnel. A few nights before, I would've heard the far-off moans and heartbeats of other tunnel dwellers. Tonight, there were none, and I was glad they'd moved on. After a day like the one I'd had, the sound of blood rushing against veins would be far too tempting. "It's more than principle—it's survival. I don't drink human blood."

"I know you don't. All I meant was that I'd do whatever it took to stop Samuel from taking more innocent lives. And I hope you'd do the same. Maybe drinking human blood would be different for you now. Maybe you could *try*."

"I can't," I said sharply. "You don't know what blood does to me. And I don't want you to find out."

Cora looked at me indignantly, but I didn't want to push the subject any further. "We should get some sleep," I said. I settled on the hard ground on the opposite side of the tunnel. I heard her shaky breathing, but I couldn't tell if she was shivering or crying. I didn't ask.

I closed my eyes and pressed my hand to my forehead,

a move that did nothing to ease the relentless pounding in my skull. Cora's suggestion echoed in my mind: *Drink human blood.*

Could I? I hadn't in twenty years, not since I was in New Orleans, where I'd sometimes drank the blood of four, five, ten humans a day with little thought to the consequences. I often dreamt of it, the moment when I was bent over a victim, smelling the rushing liquid iron, knowing it was about to run down my throat. Sometimes the liquid was bitter, like strong, black coffee. Sometimes it was sweet, with traces of honey and oranges. It used to be a private, perverse game of mine: to guess the taste before the blood touched my tongue. But no matter what the flavor, the result was the same: With human blood in me, I was stronger, faster.

Ruthless.

And in a way, Cora was right. In the short term, blood could be the fuel to power me in our fight against Samuel. But in the long run, it would destroy me.

I reached across the darkness and allowed my hand to graze Cora's slim fingers. She gently squeezed my hand, and together, somehow, the two of us fell asleep.

DON'T MISS THE NEW VAMPIRE DIARIES TRILOGY,
THE HUNTERS.
READ ON FOR A BITE OF THE FIRST VOLUME, PHANTOM.

lena Gilbert stepped onto a smooth expanse of grass, the spongy blades collapsing beneath her feet. Clusters of scarlet roses and violet delphiniums pushed up from the ground, while a giant canopy hung above her, twinkling with glowing lanterns. On the terrace in front of her stood two curving white marble fountains that shot sprays of water high into the air. Everything was beautiful, elegant, and somehow familiar.

This is Bloddeuwedd's palace, a voice in her head said. But when she had been here last, the field had been crowded with laughing, dancing partygoers. They were gone now, although signs of their presence remained: empty glasses littered the tables set around the edges of the lawn; a silken shawl was tossed over a chair; a lone high-heeled shoe perched on the edge of a fountain.

Something else was odd, too. Before, the scene had been lit by the hellish red light that illuminated everything in the Dark Dimension, turning blues to purples, whites to pinks, and pinks to the velvety color of blood. Now a clear light shone over everything, and a full white moon sailed calmly overhead.

A whisper of movement came from behind her, and Elena realized with a start that she wasn't alone after all. A dark figure was suddenly *there*, approaching her.

Damon.

Of course it was Damon, Elena thought with a smile. If anyone was going to appear unexpectedly before her here, at what felt like the end of the world—or at least the hour after a good party had ended—it would be Damon. God, he was so beautiful. Black on black: soft black hair, eyes black as midnight, black jeans, and a smooth leather jacket.

As their eyes met, she was so glad to see him that she could hardly breathe. She threw herself into his embrace, clasping him around the neck, feeling the lithe, hard muscles in his arms and chest.

"Damon," she said, her voice trembling for some reason. Her body was trembling, too, and Damon stroked her arms and shoulders, calming her.

"What is it, princess? Don't tell me you're afraid." He smirked lazily at her, his hands strong and steady.

"I *am* afraid," she answered.

"But what are you afraid of?"

That left her puzzled for a moment. Then, slowly, putting her cheek against his, she said, "I'm afraid that this is just a dream."

"I'll tell you a secret, princess," he said into her ear. "You and I are the only real things here. It's everything else that's the dream."

"Just you and me?" Elena echoed, an uneasy thought nagging at her, as though she were forgetting something—or someone. A fleck of ash landed on her dress, and she absently brushed it away.

"It's just the two of us, Elena," Damon said sharply. "You're mine. I'm yours. We've loved each other since the beginning of time."

Of course. That must be why she was trembling—it was joy. He was hers. She was his. They belonged together.

She whispered one word: "Yes."

Then he kissed her.

His lips were soft as silk, and when the kiss deepened, she tilted her head back, exposing her throat, anticipating the double wasp sting he'd delivered so many times.

When it didn't come, she opened her eyes questioningly. The moon was as bright as ever, and the scent of roses hung heavy in the air. But Damon's chiseled features were pale under his dark hair, and more ash had landed on the shoulders of his jacket. All at once, the little doubts that had been niggling at her came together.

Oh, no. Oh, no.

"Damon." She gasped, looking into his eyes despairingly as tears filled her own. "You can't be here, Damon. You're . . . dead."

"For more than five hundred years, princess." Damon flashed his blinding smile at her. More ash was falling around them, like a fine gray rain, the same gray ash Damon's body was buried beneath, worlds and dimensions away.

"Damon, you're . . . dead now. Not undead, but . . . gone."

"*No*, Elena . . ." He began to flicker and fade, like a dying lightbulb.

"Yes. Yes! I held you as you died. . . ." Elena was sobbing helplessly. She couldn't feel Damon's arms at all now. He was disappearing into shimmering light.

"Listen to me, Elena. . . ."

She was holding moonlight. Anguish caught at her heart.

"All you need to do is call for me," Damon's voice said. "All you need . . ."

His voice faded into the sound of wind rustling through the trees.

Elena's eyes snapped open. Through a fog she

registered that she was in a room filled with sunlight, and a huge crow was perched on the sill of an open window. The bird tilted its head to one side and gave a croak, watching her with bright eyes.

A cold chill ran down her spine. "Damon?" she whispered.

But the crow just spread its wings and flew away.

2

ear Diary,
 I AM HOME! I can hardly dare to believe it, but here I am.

I woke with the strangest feeling. I didn't know where I was and just lay here smelling the clean cotton-and-fabric-softener scent of the sheets, trying to figure out why everything looked so familiar.

I wasn't in Lady Ulma's mansion. There, I had slept nestled in the smoothest satin and softest velvet, and the air had smelled of incense. And I wasn't at the boardinghouse: Mrs. Flowers washes the bedding there in some weird-smelling herbal mixture that Bonnie says is for protection and good dreams.

And suddenly, I knew. I was home. The Guardians did it! They brought me home.

Everything and nothing has changed. It's the same room I slept in from when I was a tiny baby: my polished cherry-wood dresser and rocking chair; the little stuffed black-and-white dog Matt won at the winter carnival our junior year perched on a shelf; my rolltop desk with its cubbyholes; the ornate antique mirror above my dresser; and the Monet and Klimt posters from the museum exhibits Aunt Judith took me to in Washington, DC. Even my comb and brush are lined up neatly side by side on my dresser. It's all as it should be.

I got out of bed and used a silver letter opener from the desk to pry up the secret board in my closet floor, my old hiding place, and I found this diary, just where I hid it so many months ago. The last entry is the one I wrote before Founder's Day back in November, before I . . . died. Before I left home and never came back. Until now.

In that entry I detailed our plan to steal back my other diary, the one Caroline took from me, the one that she was planning to read aloud at the Founder's Day pageant, knowing it would ruin my life. The very next day, I drowned in Wickery

Creek and rose again as a vampire. And then I died again and returned as a human, and traveled to the Dark Dimension, and had a thousand adventures. And my old diary has been sitting right here where I left it under the closet floor, just waiting for me.

The other Elena, the one that the Guardians planted in everyone's memories, was here all these months, going to school and living a normal life. That Elena didn't write here. I'm relieved, really. How creepy would it be to see diary entries in my handwriting and not remember any of the things they recounted? Although that might have been helpful. I have no idea what everyone else in Fell's Church thinks has been happening in the months since Founder's Day.

The whole town of Fell's Church has been given a fresh start. The kitsune destroyed this town out of sheer malicious mischief. Pitting children against their parents, making people destroy themselves and everyone they loved.

But now none of it ever happened.

If the Guardians made good on their word, everyone else who died is now alive again: poor Vickie Bennett and Sue Carson, murdered by Katherine and Klaus and Tyler Smallwood back in the winter; disagreeable Mr. Tanner; those innocents that the kitsune killed or caused to be killed. Me. All back again, all starting over.

And, except for me and my closest friends— Meredith, Bonnie, Matt, my darling Stefan, and Mrs. Flowers—no one else knows that life hasn't gone on as usual ever since Founder's Day.

We've all been given another chance. We did it. We saved everyone.

Everyone except Damon. He saved us, in the end, but we couldn't save him. No matter how hard we tried or how desperately we pleaded, there was no way for the Guardians to bring him back. And vampires don't reincarnate. They don't go to Heaven, or Hell, or any kind of afterlife. They just . . . disappear.

Elena stopped writing for a moment and took a deep breath. Her eyes filled with tears, but she bent over the diary again. She had to tell the whole truth if there was going to be any point to keeping a diary at all.

Damon died in my arms. It was agonizing to watch him slip away from me. But I'll never let Stefan know how I truly felt about his brother. It would be cruel—and what good would it do now?

> *I still can't believe he's gone. There was no one*
> *as alive as Damon—no one who loved life more*
> *than he did. Now he'll never know—*

At that moment the door of Elena's bedroom suddenly flew open, and Elena, her heart in her throat, slammed the diary shut. But the intruder was only her younger sister, Margaret, dressed in pink flower-printed pajamas, her corn-silk hair standing straight up in the middle like a thrush's feathers. The five-year-old didn't decelerate until she was almost on top of Elena—and then she launched herself at her through the air.

She landed squarely on her older sister, knocking the breath out of her. Margaret's cheeks were wet, her eyes shining, and her little hands clutched at Elena.

Elena found herself holding on just as tightly, feeling the weight of her sister, inhaling the sweet scent of baby shampoo and Play-Doh.

"I missed you!" Margaret said, her voice on the verge of sobbing. "Elena! I missed you so much!"

"What?" Despite her effort to make her voice light, Elena could hear it shaking. She realized with a jolt that she hadn't seen Margaret—*really* seen her—for more than eight months. But Margaret couldn't know that. "You missed me so much since bedtime that you had to come running to find me?"

Margaret drew slightly away from Elena and stared at her. Margaret's five-year-old clear blue eyes had a look in them, an intensely *knowing* look, that sent a shiver down Elena's spine.

But Margaret didn't say a word. She simply tightened her grip on Elena, curling up and letting her head rest on Elena's shoulder. "I had a bad dream. I dreamed you left me. You went *away*." The last word was a quiet wail.

"Oh, Margaret," Elena said, hugging her sister's warm solidity, "it was only a dream. I'm not going anywhere." She closed her eyes and held on to Margaret, praying her sister had truly only had a nightmare, and that she hadn't slipped through the cracks of the Guardians' spell.

"All right, cookie, time to get a move on," said Elena after a few moments, gently tickling Margaret's side. "Are we going to have a fabulous breakfast together? Shall I make you pancakes?"

Margaret sat up then and gazed at Elena with wide blue eyes. "Uncle Robert's making waffles," she said. "He *always* makes waffles on Sunday mornings. Remember?"

Uncle Robert. Right. He and Aunt Judith had gotten married after Elena had died. "Sure, he does, bunny," she said lightly. "I just forgot it was Sunday for a minute."

Now that Margaret had mentioned it, she could hear someone down in the kitchen. And smell something delicious cooking. She sniffed. "Is that *bacon*?"

Margaret nodded. "Race you to the kitchen!"

Elena laughed and stretched. "Give me a minute to wake all the way up. I'll meet you down there." *I'll get to talk to Aunt Judith again,* she realized with a sudden burst of joy.

Margaret bounced out of bed. At the door, she paused and looked back at her sister. "You really are coming down, right?" she asked hesitantly.

"I really am," Elena said, and Margaret smiled and headed down the hall.

Watching her, Elena was struck once more by what an amazing second chance—third chance, really—she'd been given. For a moment Elena just soaked in the essence of her dear, darling home, a place she'd never thought she'd live in again. She could hear Margaret's light voice chattering away happily downstairs, the deeper rumble of Robert answering her. She was so *lucky*, despite everything, to be back home at last. What could be more wonderful?

Her eyes filled with tears and she closed them tightly. What a *stupid* thing to think. What could be more wonderful? If the crow on her windowsill had been Damon, if she'd known that he was out there somewhere, ready to flash his lazy smile or even purposely aggravate her, now *that* would have been more wonderful.

Elena opened her eyes and blinked hard several times, willing the tears away. She couldn't fall apart. Not now. Not when she was about to see her family again. Now she would smile and laugh and hug her family. Later she would collapse, indulging the sharp ache inside her, and let herself sob. After all, she had all the time in the world to mourn Damon, because losing him would never, ever stop hurting.

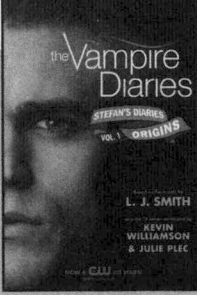
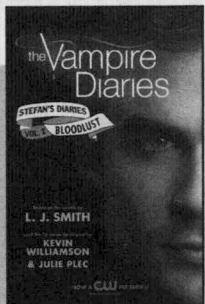